A

PROMISE

OF

TORMENT

MALLORY FOX

Mallory fox ♥

A Promise of Torment
(A Violent Agenda Book Three)

Copyright © Feb 2022 by Mallory Fox

Published in the United Kingdom by
Black Jade Publishing Ltd.

This is a work of fiction. Names, characters, businesses, places, events and incidents are either the products of the author's imagination or used in a fictitious manner. Any resemblance to actual persons, living or dead, or actual events is purely coincidental.

Editing by Indie Hub
Cover Design by Vicious Desires Design

To Jasper.
Thank you for coming into the world and making it brighter. And thanks for the stones and sticks as presents, and the fur you leave over all my clothes.

MALLORY FOX

A Promise of Torment

Blood hides carnal desires. Power is overrated.
Killing for Family is tainted with nothing but love...

My emotions are supposed to be dead.

I was never meant to feel this. Pain. Anger. **Rage**. Feelings erode me from the inside.
They make me weak. They make him more powerful.

But I can't lose.

Dante is my sweetness in hell. My father has me where he wants me. And my boys...well they think I'm all but lost.

They're right. I'm not the same Angel of Death they knew and desired. I'm losing control one promise at a time. I'm spiraling, de-evolving, turning into him.

But in the end, I need no one.
Pain, torture, and torment
is the only way to be monstrous.

I've known it all along.
Haven't you?

AUTHOR'S NOTE

A Promise of Torment is a serial killer romance intended for
mature audiences. Some scenes contain graphic violence and
potentially triggering moments. A list of all triggers can be found
at malloryfoxauthor.com. Please read at your own discretion.

Love & All Things Dark,
Mallory

GLOSSARY

The Organization a.k.a. 'The Five'

Lorcan James Duke *(formerly Joseph Duke)*

Albert Marques

Royden Earlshore

Kristian Vice *(formerly Liam 'Minotaur' Vice)*

Graham 'Griffin' Baron

The Harper-Black Family

(in Order of Inheritance)

Adrien Harper-Black *(married to Rebecca Hawkes)*

Viola Hawkes

Lily Hawkes *(daughter of Alex Hawkes)*

The Duke Family

(in Order of Inheritance)

Gordon 'Grandaddy' Duke *(married to Francesca 'Frankie' Gainsborough)*

Joseph Duke *(married to Katia Jayne Roweport)*

Tatiana Duke‡ *(married to Carl Marques)*

Byron Saint Marques† *(son of Tatiana Duke)*

Lorcan James Duke*

London Alaric Marques *(son of Tatiana Duke)*

Saskia Evelyn Duke*

The Marques Family

(in Order of Inheritance)

Albert 'Old Boy' Marques *(married to Fiona Grayson)*

~~Carl Marques~~ *(married to Tatiana Duke)*,

Jake Marques‡ *(married to Polly Leigh)*

~~Byron Saint Marques†~~

Jude Luther Marques *(son of Jake Marques)*

London Alaric Marques

Cecilia 'Cece' Grace Marques

~~Aurora May Marques~~

The Earlshore Family

(in Order of Inheritance)

Royden Earlshore *(married to Melissa 'Mimi' Derby)*

Carlotta Earlshore

The Vice Family

(in Order of Inheritance)

~~Harry Vice~~ *(married to Lola 'Birdie' Donovan)*

Kristian Vice *(married to ~~Nancy Haines~~)*

Kardinal 'Dino' Vice

Sorrow Vice *(daughter of Zeta Donovan)*

The Baron Family

(in Order of Inheritance)

Graham 'Griffin' Baron *(remarried to Lettie Knightly)*

~~Kenneth 'Midas' Baron†~~ *(divorced from Dahlia Donovan)*

Bea Baron‡ *(divorced from Charlie Havemeyer)*

Jackie Baron‡ *(married to Orion Montford)*

Finlay Baron *(son of Kenneth Baron)*

Royce Montford *(son of Jackie Baron)*

Pascal Havemeyer *(daughter of Bea Baron)*

† missing or presumed dead, * adopted, ‡ inheritance skipped or repudiated

ONE

VIOLA

NO BLOOD.

None at all.

Only the acrid smell of burning flesh tinged with copper. It fills the room with a vile stench, until Ethan drops the hot poker, face pale and bloodless like he's seen a ghost. Or a devil...One with a smile demonic enough to make a girl shiver all the way down her fucking spine.

How should I feel seeing him standing there? Grateful? Elated? Relieved? I have no idea. Peace settles over me almost at once as Dante strides forward like a hurricane, picks up the fallen poker, and shoves it right through Ethan in a beautiful arc of vengeance.

As Ethan cries out and falls back, Gigi lunges for her gun.

She's too slow.

Dante knocks her into the forge. She falls hands first into the fire, dropping the gun, rebounding with a snarl. Dante calmly slams her head into the wall until she's out cold. Ethan, spitting blood and curses from where he is on the floor, isn't quite dead. But I'm too absorbed in Dante leaning over me to care.

His cologne envelopes my senses. Excitement snakes through my body, bringing me back to life. As he rips away my bonds like they're nothing but candy floss, I don't breathe or move. Dante is an enigma. I've no idea what he's going to do. Thankfully, he steps back allowing me up. If he'd have so much as tried to gather me in his arms, I would have bitten his fucking ear off.

I don't waste any time. I throw myself off the table with an inhuman growl until I'm straddling Ethan, and then yank the poker from his body. Dante missed his heart and any vitals. No, he's definitely not dead...yet.

Dante left him for me.

I shove the still-hot poker straight through Ethan's eye, melting half his face off. His screams are beautiful. I'll relish that sound forever and a day. When I'm done, I stagger to my feet only to then stumble right back down again.

Fuck. I'm actually in a lot of pain.

Too much pain to play happy rescue with my not-so-would-be hero.

*Dante rescuing me...*I snort a laugh as I breathe, and then wince as I move my legs in front of me. Searing agony blooms across my burnt thigh. Dante's eyes narrow as he watches me just sitting on the floor laughing. Then his eyes sweep to the area where Ethan desecrated my flesh with daddy's fucking company logo. *Like I'm his fucking property.*

"Don't tell me you need me to carry you up the stairs, V. You weigh a ton," Dante says casually. Though I don't miss the tic in his jaw and the balling of his fist by his side.

"Fuck off. Touch me and I'll make you wish you were dead," I say as my chest restricts and my teeth grind. I pick myself up off the tiled stone floor for a second time and survey the damage.

Gigi is out cold. Ethan is dead.

It's just me and Dante left.

Dante. I know he has a gun on him. I stare at my ex-mentor and assess his intentions. *Why the fuck is he helping me? He was the one who brought me here and left me. He dumped me here for a reason.*

What does helping me now achieve? I did offer to pay him for killing my father, but that kind of money isn't easy to come by, and I haven't paid him yet. He must know I don't have it.

And if he is helping me, can we shoot our way out of here with one fucking gun?

"Your father went to his office. There's no one else in this part of the building," my mentor says, reading my mind like his own. Then he departs upstairs, moving silently like a goddamn cat.

I step over a prone and motionless Ethan and limp up the stairs, out of the fucking basement, and after Dante with as much pride as I can manage. He's waiting when I get to the top with barely veiled fucking amusement teasing his lips. I ignore him and locate the first aid kit. There should be something in there for a burn—cream or a cooling gel of some sort. I sense him lean against the wall, watching me toss the contents of the kit onto the counter. His attention switches over to the far side of the room where the door is before coming back again, ever alert.

Finally, I find what I'm looking for. I give a sigh of relief and part my skirt, exposing my leg. Only then do I glance at Dante.

His gaze locks with mine. His mouth is still curled into a bow-like smirk which just annoys the fuck out of me.

"You think this is funny," I say to him, looking up into his usually emotionless blue eyes. Dante's dead blue eyes are actually sparkling. "Am I hilarious to you?"

"No, I think you're pretty perfect."

His reply isn't what I expected and it throws me. *What do I say to that? Do I make a joke? Do I tell him to go fuck himself?*

Pretty perfect.

What does that even mean? I have a fucking 'H' branded into my skin. How am I fucking perfect? I turn away from him and take some hardcore painkillers before putting the burn cream on, slathering it all over my thigh.

After a minute or two, the cooling ointment has soothed a little of the raw edges inside and out. Dante is a good ally to have. I shouldn't alienate him, not when I've been trying my damnedest to win the bastard over.

"So, what now?" I say, letting out a breath to calm my nerves, mind picking over the pieces of what happened. I keep my gaze on where he has a gun hidden, glancing up at his face briefly to assess his intentions.

"V, this is your show. I'm just back-up," he shrugs.

"You never take a contract without payment upfront. I haven't paid you yet."

Dante cocks his head, hands in his pockets, an annoying smile still on his lips. "Haven't you?"

I snort. "You know I haven't."

"My bad. I'll just have to collect from you later then," he says, staring into my eyes, bleeding me dry with the intensity of that damned gaze of his.

"Maybe you could collect now," I say tilting my head, licking my lips, bunching my skirt up higher.

I've never flirted with Dante.

Never.

But I'm riding high on adrenaline right now, so anything fucking goes. Dante's eyes darken and his brows pinch in the middle.

"What?" I give a soft laugh. "You can come into the kitchen, but you can't take the heat?" Dante flirted first, at least that's what I'm telling myself. This isn't weird, is it? We grew up together. My father practically adopted him after his parents died. I've never liked Dante in any other way but as a big brother…

Until now.

I let go of the hem of my skirt and push away from the table I'm leaning against, slightly unsteady. The painkillers are taking effect. I can hardly feel the sting anymore. It could also be the excitement of what I'm about to do drowning everything else out.

Did I ever mention how absolutely beautiful Dante is? Probably not.

I try to ignore the way he looks because the Devil shouldn't appear to be so divine.

Icy blue eyes look down at me under hooded lids. Blond hair, tousled and messy, snatched back at the nape of his neck. I've always wondered how it would feel running my hands through his hair.

Is it soft? Does it smell of him?

I walk up to Dante, looking at him with new eyes. And when I'm in front of him and he towers over me, my hand reaches up and teases a lock of it—his hair. It's softer than mine—feathery and delicate like the wings of a fucking angel.

"V, what's going on?" my ex-mentor asks.

Cheekbones that could slice through veins. Stubble that sculpts his chin. Full cupid-bow lips that beg to be kissed. I know from past gigs when we've shared hotel rooms that he has a butterfly tattoo on his chiseled chest. He never told me what it meant. I trace the outline of it now through his t-shirt.

"Men don't rescue me. I rescue myself. When it does happen, I must admit it's a huge turn-on. I'm practically frothing at the mouth for a real man to take control of me," I say.

The boys were wrong.

Dante is the Angel of Death, not me.

With a sigh, I lean in and rest my head on his chest.

"V," he warns. There's so much warning in that one letter.

Dante is every girl's wet fucking dream.

Too bad…I hate him.

I pull back. Dante's gun is in my hands. I point it at his head. The look on his face is worth it.

"What did you say earlier? Pretty damn perfect?" I say. "Mind if I borrow this for a while?"

"You don't want to do this," he says, blue eyes dark and unreadable.

"Didn't you say this was my show?"

He holds up his hands, mouth twitching at the corners. "You still don't trust me?"

"Trust is earned, not bought," I say. "Now, where is Adrien?"

"I told you. He's in the other building. But I wouldn't try this alone if I were you."

I narrow my eyes and snort. "What are you talking about? I do every fucking thing alone."

I usher Dante back into the basement stairwell and lock him in. Then I cease worrying about him and make my way to the other building to find my father.

There are two parts to his estate. The main house, and my father's office when he's not in the city. Dante could be telling the truth. Why would he lie? Still, I don't fancy going to kill my father without a weapon and with Dante at my back.

Once I put a bullet in Adrien's head, I'm walking away from this fucked-up life. I'm so done with this bullshit. I don't even care about my family name, or fortune. The government can take it all. Asking Dante to kill my father was a mistake. I know that now. No one can kill the bastard but me. It has to be me. As it was always meant to be.

I'm better off alone.

I need no one.

Outside my father's office is an empty corridor. That's strange. Where are his men? There should be someone here at all times, or at least that's how it was when I lived here. I shudder at the memory. It was a long time ago, but it feels like yester-fucking-day.

Fuck, the drugs have kicked in, but not fast enough.

Gingerly, trying not to wince, I stalk toward the office. On the other side of the door, I can hear him talking to someone, so I know he's in there. I promised my mother before she broke down that I was never coming back. This place was my history, not my fucking future. I'm doing this for her, and for me. I'm doing this to be free.

Kicking down doors in reality never fucking works, so I open the door the normal way. It swings wide and I see him as he sees me. He's behind his desk on the phone. As soon as our eyes connect, he pauses mid-sentence to whoever he's talking to.

"Hello, Adrien," I say, stepping into the room, keeping the gun aimed right at him. He doesn't react, so I stop halfway in. Adrenaline spikes and inside I'm holding back a scream. Dante trained me to be ruthless.

So this is what I'm being.

"Do it," he says, in a soft, dangerous voice. It's the voice that gave me nightmares for years. I stare at him and will myself to end him for good.

I don't hesitate to kill. It's not who I am, but with him staring at me, I'm frozen in place. All the monsters I've tried to escape, my past, my tormentors, are embodied in him. All the hate and rage, my own monster that comes creeping, stem from him.

Killing him is easier said than done. I readjust my grip on the gun, ignoring the rise of panic making it slick in my trembling in my hands.

He snorts. "You can't, can you?"

"Oh I can," I say, sucking in a breath, pulling the damn trigger. "Goodbye, Father."

It's the first and last time I'll ever call him that to his face.

TWO

VIOLA

NOTHING HAPPENS.

The chamber clicks like it's empty.

I try again.

Click, click, click.

My father takes me in as he puts his phone down. "My ever predictable, useless daughter. Did you steal that pistol from Dante?"

My senses heighten. Adrenaline rushing through me in waves. I eye his desk. There's a fountain pen next to his notepad. I could throw the gun at him, snatch the pen, and shove it into his throat. That would stop him from talking. There's nothing to stop me from doing all that, so why do I feel like this is a trap?

The gun hasn't jammed. It has no bullets.

He follows my gaze. "Are you thinking of using the pen?" He leans back. "Well, go ahead. Take your best shot. But I warn you, it'll be your downfall."

Reluctantly, I lower my aim and glare at him. "What am I missing?"

"You're smarter than you look," he says nodding, eyes

averting to look over my shoulder as the door opens behind me. "But not smart enough."

I know it's Dante behind me because he doesn't make a sound after the door closes shut. Still, I can't help but turn around to make sure.

Yep. It's him. The fuckwit.

I glare at Dante, and he cocks a brow when he sees the gun dangling in my hand at my side. "I told you not to do this alone, but you wouldn't listen."

"Fuck off," I snap. My one chance at killing Adrien just got smaller. Minuscule, in fact.

"Now that we're all here, let's get down to business. Sit." My father orders, gesturing to the chairs in front of his desk. I don't move. I'd rather stand. "I said sit, the both of you."

Dante walks past me and takes a seat. After a few minutes, I do the same. I keep the gun in my lap even though it's empty of bullets. I hate guns, but they're a comfort when you're surrounded by snakes.

I glance at Dante. He appears relaxed, but who knows what's going on inside his head. *Why ever did I think he was hot?*

"Do you know what I've always said?" Adrien says.

"I've no fucking idea," I retort, and I don't.

"Loyalty is what makes family," Adrien says. "And as much as I would love to embrace my own daughter as family, it seems you still have a lot to learn."

"We were never a family. You made sure of that." My father has always seen me and my mother as tools, assets, things to be owned and used. Family is a fucking illusion.

Adrien frowns, pressing his lips together. "Have you quite finished?"

I stare back at him coldly. "Just tell me what your game is."

He sneers. "My game? You think this is a game, child?" His use of the word child makes me snort. "What's so amusing?"

"Children are innocent. *I* never have been. Now tell me what the fuck is going on or I walk. Fuck family."

He regards me with blank eyes, leaning back. "This was a test," he says finally. "Dante here trained you, but I believed you to be weak. Ethan branding you was to see how you'd react." He looks to Dante.

"She killed Ethan, and stole my gun," Dante shrugs.

My father considers this. "Just Ethan?"

When Dante affirms, he returns his focus to me. "Why didn't you try to kill Dante?"

I know the answer. I know what I should say. But fuck him if I'm playing ball. "I'm done with this," I hiss, getting to my feet. I shoot Dante a look of pure disgust. He played me and I hate him even more for it. I should have known that I couldn't trust him. Test my goddamn ass.

"Sit down or I'll make you," Adrien warns.

"Fuck you," I retort.

My father sighs. "Dante, make the bitch sit."

I get as far as the door when I feel Dante's arm around my neck, and a hand through my hair, jerking me backward. *Fucking hell, I didn't even hear him move.* I try to headbutt him, but he tightens his grip, dragging me back into the room by my roots. I struggle in silence as he does, the feeling of my hair being yanked out making my eyes water. "Play along, V, he has Rebecca," Dante says softly in my ear.

I stop moving at that.

Rebecca. My mother.

"Are you done?" Dante says louder. I nod and he lets me go.

I spin around, hair wild about my face where the fuckwit half pulled it out. I stare at Dante, but his face is devoid of emotion. Un-fucking-readable. *What the fuck...where is she?* I want to demand it of both of them. But I don't. If my father doesn't want me to know about my mother, then me knowing that means I have something over him. It does explain why Dante is being an obedient dog, though I'm still pissed at him.

"I grow tired of your outbursts," Adrien says. "Sit the fuck down or I'll lose my patience." He gestures to the chairs again.

I suck in a breath, soothing my beast. My vision is red, but my mind is all black. Finally, I sit and so does Dante.

"Now, let's start again, shall we. It's time for you to take your place as my heir."

I'm not listening. I'm concentrating on what I'm going to do to him once I find Rebecca. His lips move but I hear none of the words that come out. It's only when Dante grabs my hand and leads me out of my father's office do I snap out of it.

I should kill him. Dante.

He betrayed me and fucked me off for the last time. Rage has slowly been corroding my veins until all I can do is not explode.

"Don't," Dante hisses at me, hauling me down the corridor, prizing the gun from my frozen hands. "Not here. He's watching. Play nice."

Play nice? You fucking bastard. Dante was the only one who could find her and deliver her to my father. While I was playing fucking house with Lorcan, Jude, and Dino...Dante was burying me and my mother alive.

He leads me into a room further down the hall. I recognize it as soon as we're inside. It's Dante's room when he stays here. He grabs my face, making me look at him, but all I can do is let the monster stare back. Fuck keeping it under wraps. We're alone now.

I know I need Dante. That he can be the perfect ally. But right now, I also want him dead. *I want him hurting like I am.*

The monster in me wins and I scream as I launch myself at him, trying to bite a hole in his fucking chest, trying to carve his heart out with my damn teeth.

Pain explodes in my skull dropping me to the floor in an instant.

"You mother fucker," I say in a low voice as I struggle to get to my feet. The last thing I see is Dante holding his gun by the barrel before he crashes me over the head with the butt of it, again.

· · ·

Voices. Male voices.

They sound familiar. A deep lull that brings me back to life like a moth to a flame. I flutter my eyes open to take in my surroundings. *Where the fuck am I?*

Someone reaches over to brush my hair—a loving touch. *Don't fucking touch me.* I jerk my hand up to hit away whoever just invaded my personal space and come up short. My hands are tied in front of me and attached to the bed—my bed.

I'm in my bedroom, and I'm not alone.

The adrenaline screams through my body as I throw myself against my bonds, turning my head to half sit up and see who the fuck is touching me without my permission.

Forest green eyes, filled with judgment, regard me from above —Lorcan.

My nostrils flare as I shift my gaze left to see Dino behind him, peering at me with concern etched all over his face. *What the hell are they doing here?* Breathing hard, I throw myself into a sitting position. Well as much as I can with my hands tied the way they are. My head throbs and the inside of my mouth feels like sandpaper. The last thing I need is the two of them here and now.

"What are you doing here?" I say, clearing my throat and licking my lips to moisten them. I can taste blood on them. My neck feels stiff as I try to adjust my legs. "Can you fucking untie me?"

Lorcan, eyes full of distrust, doesn't bother to move. He just blinks at me from the side of the bed where he's sitting. "So you can run off again? Fuck no, you're going to answer some questions first."

I dart my gaze to Dino, appealing to the weakest link.

"Lorcan's right," Dino says with a sigh.

I arch a brow, glaring between the two of them from where I'm trussed up on the mattress.

"Are you serious?" I say.

"Completely," says Lorcan.

"Fine. Just tell me how you got in here."

"We tailed Dante. The bastard found us and brought us here. You were out cold when we found you."

"Dante brought you here?" I say in disbelief. "Why would he do that?

"Oh, no you don't. We're asking the questions, not you." Lorcan's tone is practically scathing.

I blink at him. "Fine. Untie me and I'll tell you what you want to know." I lift my hands up.

Lorcan looks at me, and then folds his arms.

Fuck you then. I switch my attention to Dino. I don't miss his gaze avert to Lorcan. Fucking pussy. "Grow a pair, Vice, why don't you," I snort. He hesitates for a few seconds, but then comes over and starts undoing the tape around my wrists.

"Good boy," I say, patting Dino on the cheek when my wrists are free. Dino gives me a sorrowful look, like I'm utterly doomed. Then he shakes his head and steps away from me, like I'm some kind of monster.

Dante had the tape tight. I suppress the urge to rub my wrists and instead glare at Lorcan. He's still upset, but there's a flash of something else—fear.

"Okay what is it? Why are you both creeping around me like I'm some kind of animal?"

"Have you looked in the mirror lately?" Lorcan drawls.

I narrow my eyes and then sit up higher so I can see myself in the dressing table mirror at the end of the bed. My hair is all over the place and my pupils are large, making my eyes bigger. But that's not why the boys are scared.

Blood stains coat my mouth and lips. My reflection is a vision of hell.

It makes me grin, and the wild girl in the mirror gives me an insane looking smile back with dark red teeth.

Then it comes back to me. I bit Dante right where his heart was. Did I damage his butterfly? Maim a wing? The giggle escapes me before I can stop it.

"It's not funny, Viola," Dino sighs.

"Oh, bloody hell. Do you really think I'm going to bite you?" I say to both of them.

Lorcan cocks his head. "I wouldn't put anything past you. You're acting like a crazy bitch right now."

"I thought you liked that," I say, licking my finger and smearing the blood over my lips and then sucking my finger clean. Lorcan's eyes bulge out of his head, and Dino's complexion gets whiter than I've ever seen it, and he's pale as fuck being a redhead.

THREE

VIOLA

I CRAWL on my hands and knees across the bed towards Lorcan, who doesn't move a muscle—if you don't count the one in his jaw.

When my face is inches from his, I lick his cheek and slip one hand down his waistband to his cock. I'm pleasantly surprised to find him rock hard for me. I stroke him with my nails, but he doesn't react, so I use those nails to dig into his balls. He just glares like he's disappointed in me.

It only makes the darkness want to hurt him more.

But I rein it in....*just*.

"What? You don't want to kiss me now?" I say cocking my head, teasing the length of him until a little pre-cum comes out.

It doesn't take much. Lorcan grabs me and kisses me, tasting blood and all. I devour him. I've been starved of physical contact for far too long it seems. I wrap my arms around his neck, but he pushes me off him, back onto the bed. "Watch it. I was just in a car crash in case you forgot. I'm on top."

I grin as he straddles me. I'll let him take control, but I want my pound of flesh. He bends down to claim my mouth again, slower this time. As he undoes his trousers, I claw at his back and bite his neck. Not too hard, but he pulls back.

"No biting or scratching, or I tape you back up," he growls.

"Why do you have to make it so boring?" I say. His gaze darkens at that. He takes my wrists and forces them above my head, holding them with one hand, then he tears at my thin panties, ripping them aside.

I try to move, to scratch him, but he's got me where he wants me. My breathing quickens as he takes his cock out and presses it against my entrance.

"Am I still boring you, or have I got your full attention?" he asks, raw emotion burning in the depths of his eyes.

"You've got me. What are you going to do now?" I say, taunting him.

His lips make a sly smile. Then he slams into me, brutally, perfectly, fully, making me gasp. Lorcan isn't small, and I'm not ready for him even if I am drenched.

Behind him, Dino takes in the scene, fear, and lust dancing in his baby blue eyes. He frees his cock from his jeans, moving his hand up and down his own hardening shaft. The sight of him getting off on watching us has my whole body on fire.

Lorcan continues to drill into me, pounding me like he can't quite control himself. Not that I have any control left, my moans and bucks are all that's left of me. Lorcan was right to hold me down. I don't know what I'd do if I was on top.

The orgasm ravages my body as pleasure rushes over me in waves.

"That's it, sweetheart, come for me," Lorcan drawls.

I close my eyes and let Lorcan take my release. I need him to right the pain inside before it erodes away what's left. I savaged Dante with my teeth. I wanted to. I wanted to taste his flesh in my mouth and swallow it down. I wanted to hear him fucking scream my name while I devoured him, in more ways than one.

What scares me the most is not that I enjoyed it…

But I was totally in control.

"Enjoy that sweetheart?" Lorcan drawls, as he leans down to bite my shoulder. He said no biting but I'm not a pussy like he is, so I don't tell him to stop. I'm too busy riding the ecstasy of a waning orgasm.

"Is that all you've got," I ask after a pause, panting lightly. He smirks, pulling back. My body twists and grinds against his. No! I want more.

I need more.

Locan's eyes glint in the darkness. "That's all you're getting. Now it's our turn to fill you up."

I glare at him as he holds me down and shoves his full length into me, making me gasp. Then he fucks me savagely. His pace is somewhere between heaven and hell, lighting me on fire. He uses me like I used him, until his cock swells and he thrusts hard and deep one last time.

"Fuck," he growls as he jerks, spilling his release inside me. A second wave of pleasure rips through me, unexpectedly, intense and desperate as the first. Lorcan shudders over me with a sigh, kissing me briefly on the lips before he whips his head to Dino, who looks about to come himself. "Don't waste it. Give her what she wants," Lorcan says.

Dino's eyes darken but he nods and groans, pumping furiously, throwing his head back as he steps forward and empties his hot load over my stomach and breasts.

Lorcan, still pinning me to the bed, smears it over me and then rubs a generous amount on my lips. "Don't ever say you're bored when I'm fucking you," he sneers.

His finger comes too close to my teeth. I snap at him but he manages to pull his hand away unscathed.

"Fucking asshole," I scowl.

After, I lay in the sheets, skirt strewn up around my waist, Dino quickly disappears into the bathroom and Lorcan climbs off me and fixes himself. The back of his neck has raised welts where my nails dug in. Lorcan turns around. His eyes are shuttered, closed off to me again. I've hurt him by pushing him away, and now he's punishing me by doing the same.

"Are you coming home?" Lorcan asks, not even bothering to look at me as he tucks himself back into his trousers.

It's like that then, is it?

"I am home," I say.

Lorcan scowls and stalks toward the bathroom to clean up. I should clean up too. I can feel his cum leaking out from between my legs and onto the bed. I'm covered in Dino's too. The feel of it sliding over my skin arouses me, so I turn my focus to my sweet Dino, who is exiting the bathroom as Lorcan goes in. He takes me in with hungry eyes. I doubt his hand satisfied him enough. I moisten my lips, tasting him, and give him a come-hither look.

I'm still starved.

I need more.

"Come here," I say, patting the bed next to me.

Dino shakes his head, looking absolutely disgusted with himself. In his hands is a towel. He takes a step closer, offering it to me.

I ignore his gesture. I'm broken, may as well be dirty too.

"This isn't why we came," he says, putting the towel on the bed next to me but still keeping me at arm's length.

The laugh rises and sticks in my throat. "But you did come. Both of you," I say, making eyes at him.

Suddenly, he hisses.

"What—" He strides forward and lifts my skirt, exposing the brand Ethan gave me. "—happened? Who hurt you? Dante?" he exclaims.

I glance down. The wound is no longer visible. It's dressed in a white gauze which is stained red with blood. All that fucking must have made it weep. It's not very discreet. They must have been too preoccupied to notice before. I shrug. "Adrien," is the only word I say.

"Your fucking father did that to you?" He's cute when his nostrils flare and his dimple appears out of nowhere.

"He ordered one of his men to. It's fine. Stop fussing."

Dino runs a hand through his hair. "And you want to still stay here? I don't get you, Viola. Why? Why not come home?" His eyes plead with me to give him an answer he understands.

I could tell him about my mother. I could explain that running away again won't fix my past. That I need to finish this. The darkness demands it. My stained soul needs it. I'm sick and tired of running. All this time I killed other perverts for vengeance, when the real monster was in my blood.

My fucking father…

But I don't say any of this. Dino turned his back on his family long ago. Lorcan is adopted. Jude paid me to kill his family off. They would never understand the pull of familial ties.

Of blood.

I sit up and stare into Dino's wounded eyes. He's close enough for me to reach for him, but I don't. He still has his hands on my thigh, branding me where he holds me with his own kind of pain.

Love taints all it touches.

And that's why I have to burn it all down to the fucking ground.

"Let me be clear," I say. "I am home. This is where I belong. It was fun to play vigilante with you boys for a while, but now I need to go back to being a grown up."

"What about the plan?"

"Screw the plan. I'm a hired gun not a charity worker. I killed for each one of you. Joseph. Carl. Even Mr. Hands. You had me for a month to take care of your teacher problem. I did what I could, with no fucking reward, and look where it got me!" I snap, gesturing at the burn on my leg.

"So, what are you saying? That we were nothing but a distraction?"

I give Dino a cruel smile, even as my internal world tilts on its axis. "There. You got it. That wasn't so hard, was it? Now it's your turn to keep your promise. I killed for you. You owe me. So go and do your fucking job." My throat feels raw as I say it. Like I've been screaming for hours without relenting.

"But fuck, Viola…I love you," Dino chokes, blue eyes glistening wet like he's about to fucking cry. "We all do."

The darkness sucks me down and I let it.

"I never said it," I say. "I've never once said I love you. You were just a bit of fun. A distraction for a while."

My words sound empty as I say them. Dino's blue eyes seem shut down, closing off to me as he takes them in.

It's true, I craved them. But I used them to keep my monster in check. And I can be whimsical at times. I go where my stone-cold heart takes me. But all roads lead to torment eventually. To quote Dante—*Nothing lasts. Dreams end. People fucking die.* Seeing Lorcan on that hospital bed was a wake-up call. My monster needs other monsters to handle it. If I stay with the boys, I will kill them in the end.

Not Dante.

Not their families.

Me.

Lorcan, Dino, and even Jude aren't demons…even if they pretend to be. They're saints, sinners at most.

Only the demons can love me.

And only I can deal with the Devil alone.

After Lorcan and Dino leave, I shower and change, and take a handful of painkillers. My head is no longer killing me, but my thigh has started throbbing again. My insides are a mess too. Dino shot a regretful look at me over his shoulder as he left. Guilt is not something I usually have to deal with, so call me confused at the shitty feeling rampaging through my gut right now.

I did the right thing, letting them go. I'm no good for them. Lorcan was nearly killed. Jude is in prison. All because of me.

So why do I feel so cold and empty?

I'm just tired. I need to sleep more.

The sun has set and it's past midnight when I finally head to Dante's room. I must have been out of it most of the day. I don't knock. I barge in. Dante is shirtless wearing only a pair of sweats and fingerless training gloves doing fucking sit-ups or something that requires steel-hard abs.

He stops working his body—already slick with sweat—as soon as he sees me and rests back on one arm, using the other to bring his water bottle to his lips. He jerks his chin up. "Close the door, you're letting the heat in."

All the windows are open, making his room into a frigid cell. I forgot that Dante loves the cold. It makes him feel alive, he once told me. I guess you have to go to extreme lengths when you're virtually dead on the inside.

I perch on the end of his bed, noting the white patch of gauze on his chest, above his pec where the wing tip of the butterfly tattoo is.

"So, I didn't dream it? I really did bite a hole in your chest?"

Dante shrugs, all super languid as he lounges on the floor. Thank fuck. I couldn't take another cry baby. "You were upset and needed an outlet," he says.

"You don't appear to be upset about it."

"Better my chest than my balls."

He's got a point.

"How bad is it?"

"A few teeth marks. Will probably scar." He takes a sip of his water. "I've had worse."

"How many is that now?" I ask him. Back when we were training, we used to keep tabs on how many times we scarred each other. At the last count I was winning.

His lips curl up into a smile, one that doesn't quite reach his eyes, but he looks like he's proud. "Seven," he says.

I have three from Dante. No more than that. One on my shoulder where he slipped a knife in when I tackled him. One on my arm where he sliced me with a piece of wood while sparring. And one on my middle finger where he snapped it and it had to be pinned back together with metal parts. To this day, I can't straighten it properly. I've blamed Dante for my crappy aim compared to him with a gun since then.

Still, I don't know why he stopped at three. He's had plenty of time to even out the score.

"Did you have a nice time with your schoolboys?" he asks.

"Don't be jealous, you're the one who let them in."

"They were going to get themselves killed snooping around. I just sped up the process of you ripping off the Band-aid," he says. At least he agrees with me that letting them go is for the best. Though, I'm not sure if it's a good thing, given his desire to always be alone.

I sigh and draw my knees up onto the bed, trying not to shiver. The room is ice cold. I bet if I breathed out, you'd be able to see it misting.

"If you're cold, get out," Dante says, taking another sip of water.

"Whose side are you on?" I come out and say it. I'm not one to beat about the bush.

"My own."

I give him a look. "Don't lie. You're on the side who pays the most."

"Then why ask?"

"Because I want to know if it was you who told my father where my mother was."

He gets to his feet, holding the water bottle, and walks over to where I am until he's at the edge of the bed. I unwrap my arms from my legs and casually lean back, looking up into his cold blue eyes. Despite the chilly air, he smells of sweat and cologne.

"Rebecca was like a mother to me. I would never hurt her."

"Says the killer who works for her tormentor."

"Your father pays me well. I'd be a fool to let sentiment get in the way of business," he says, looking down on me. His gaze, cold and clinical as always, stokes a flame in my very soul. No one looks at me like Dante does.

As he turns away, the cold air rushes in from where he was blocking the draught and a chill runs over me.

It dampens the fire inside too.

And I feel empty once more.

"Is that all I am to you? Fucking business?"

He picks up a shirt and throws it on, half looking back. "You've always been business, V," he says.

Dante takes a blade from his desk, twiddles it in his hand, and tosses it to me. "And a little pleasure."

I catch it. The metal is glacial in my fingers, burning its own kind of fire.

"What's this for?" I ask, frowning up at him.

Dante approaches with a couple of manila folders. He drops them on the bed next to me. They're the type of folders Polina used to send us, ones that contains all the data Quinn could ever access about a mark. Paper being 100% untraceable.

I open the first one and look inside.

"My next victim," Dante says, lips curling into an evil grin as I see who it is. "Is your next ally."

Griffin.

"I thought he was my father's business partner?"

"He is. Your father wants him gone. He's got too much control over the streets and Adrien doesn't like that. But it's what's going to give us leverage to make him ours."

Us. Ours.

Is this another test? I look at my mentor with guarded eyes. If Dante was an enigma before, he's a fucking paradox now.

"And this one?" I open it. Inside is another of my father's associates. "Is he your target too?"

"No, V, he's yours."

FOUR

VIOLA

Two Months Later:

The man I need to kill is at the blackjack table betting everything he has. It's not one of my father's business partners. It's another mark.

I've no idea who he is, except that he hasn't paid back what he owes Adrien. An insult when he clearly has the money. My father would send an idiot like this a warning first. But this guy lost that chance when he ran. Running does nobody any good. I could have told him that. Still, it's the perfect opportunity to get close to my real target.

I still don't know if this is a trap or not. But my father will kill Rebecca if I don't at least pretend to comply. And Dante is right; this is the perfect time to gain leverage. But if I trust Dante again, will he fuck me over like last time? What if this is just another test from my father to see if I'll take the bait?

I glance at the folders on the bed. "What's in it for you?" I say to Dante.

"You know I don't have the money to pay you."

After selling the jewelry Saskia gave me as payment for killing Joseph, I used most of it to pay bills. Working only for the boys, for free I might add, for the last few months has meant my funds are at an all-time low.

The last time I checked I was practically broke.

"Half your inheritance", he says without hesitation.

I narrow my eyes. "You want half of Harper-Black? Why?"

I know the answer as soon as I ask the question. I never wanted my father's estate or name, but Dante is not like me. He's not blood. He can come and go as he pleases. Adrien may have taken him in, but my father doesn't give a shit about owning him. He's a useful tool to him, nothing more.

I never thought about it before, but Dante gets nothing if my father dies. Nothing. And without a family of his own, it would be like he never existed.

Power—this is what it all boils down to. Dante may be a natural born killer, but he also has ambition. What can you give someone who has more money than sense?

Only your name.

Dante never answered my question, and I don't think I really wanted to hear his answer. Dante has always been a demon to me with one thing on his mind—spilling blood. Money, yes. But power? Prestige? That's not the Dante I know. And if it's true, I've never really understood him.

In fact, I don't know him at all.

I take a sip of my wine and study my pretend target. Dante is here somewhere too, and he'll be getting impatient with me if I don't act soon. I wish now that we'd worn earpieces. Dante hates them. He always says I should know instinctively what he's going to do by now, so he shouldn't have to tell me. Usually, I agree. But this time, the desire to interrogate him, to peel away the layers and get to know the guy I grew up with…burns beneath my skin like poison.

Because I don't know you, Dante.

And possibly never will.

As soon as my mark loses cards for a fifth time, he downs his drink, gets unsteadily to his feet, and walks in the direction of the bar. I chase away my own shitty feeling by drinking some wine. Then I discreetly leave the table, where I'm neither winning or losing, and follow him.

Thankfully, the bar is less crowded than the main floor, almost deserted. Who wants to drink when you can gamble? Just the losers drowning their sorrows. I approach the man I've been following for the better half of the night and slip into the semi-private booth next to him.

He looks pleased to see me. Of course, he does. I'm wearing a long black dress with a slit up one side, though not the side that has a H seared into my skin. My hair—a wig—is mouse brown, loose and pin straight, tucked behind one ear. I have on the lightest touches of makeup. Pink blush-colored lip gloss. A simple, silver chain around my neck. I look young, too young for this place.

I offer my target a shy smile as I order a drink with a passing waiter. He pays with money he doesn't have. I touch his arm. He leans in, complimenting me.

In five minutes flat, he's all mine.

Just like the rest of them.

His hands glide up my thigh and I resist the urge to choke him with my silver chain. The sensation of him touching me turns my stomach. This would be a great time to suggest we go somewhere a little quieter, and then skin him alive. Or just drown him in his own vomit.

But I'm not really here for that.

I plaster a smile on my face and neck my wine. Great thing about Dante not being in my fucking ear is that he can't tell me to slow down. Why would I slow down? Adrien could send anyone. Dante. Gigi. Any one of his men. But he continues to send me on high risk, low value jobs. Adrien couldn't care less about that so long as I kill the man who stole from him.

And Kato, his business partner.

The darkness inside buzzes like a wounded wasp, eating away what's left of my psyche as I look around. I see no sign of Kato or his men, but that doesn't mean they aren't watching. Although the wig and blue contacts might dissuade them from watching too closely, I am in Triad territory. Kato owns this part of the city and everyone in it. Even if I'm here on Kato's good graces, since my mother's father was a Triad and I'm the daughter of his business partner, it's usual for me to present myself first. It's only polite.

He must be watching.

I scan the room again, gnashing my teeth as the drunken guy continues to maul me, until a swathe of black hair catches my eye. He's sitting in a private booth, wearing a tailored black suit. His arm is around a leggy blonde, free hand groping up her dress. I can't see his face all too well because the blonde is sucking it off. But I'd recognize the tattoos kissing the edge of his razored fade anywhere.

It's fucking Lorcan.

I suck in a breath. Seeing him after all this time twists a dagger into my chest, which is ridiculous. It's been months since he left the estate with Dino. *I didn't even miss them when they were gone.* Well, maybe there was a small part of me that felt empty not having them around. But being a hostage of my father. I haven't given any of the boys much thought. And now he's here, letting some bitch drape herself all over him.

All I see is red.

The guy in the booth with me puts his hand up my skirt and that red turns to flame. I seize his drink, spilling alcohol over us both.

"Hey, watch it, kitten, this is an expensive suit!" he exclaims.

I smash the glass at the stem and press the pointy end against his throat. Crimson blooms where I poke it into the softest, fleshiest part.

"Don't fucking touch me," I say in a low, empty voice.

He doesn't move, whites showing in his eyes as he focuses on me. I'm lucky that the bar is empty, and no one can see me threatening to kill the bastard. Sloppy though. I should not be acting this way. I've blown my cover and now I need to extract myself before I shove the glass in deeper.

I leave the booth without killing my actual mark—ironic, I know—and make a beeline for Lorcan's table, dropping the shard of glass into a plant pot on the way there. The blonde is practically riding Lorcan at this point. Without thinking, I reach for my dagger.

"Miss Harper-Black, will you please come with me?" says a voice behind me, making me halt halfway across the bar floor.

I shift my attention to my right. My hand still rests on my dagger through the thin material of the dress but getting it won't be easy.

This has better be important.

It is.

It's one of Kato's men who works at the casino. I recognize him as the maître d of sorts. He looks down his nose at me as he waits for my answer to his question. "Kato wants to speak to you," he elaborates.

I look at him blankly and then give him a curt nod. As I follow him into one of the private corridors behind a security door, I shoot a glance at Lorcan who still has his hands full.

I'll deal with him later.

Right now, I need to know what Kato wants. He knows I'm here, but he doesn't know the real reason why. I've no idea how he'll react when he does.

"Why does my father want Kato dead?"

Dante looks at me. "That's classified."

"Bullshit. I need to know."

"No, you don't."

"Tell me," I say.

"Rebecca was having an affair with Kato."

"Since when?" My mother has been in a sanitarium for years. A

place so expensive I can hardly keep up with the payments some months. If she was having an affair, I would know about it.

"It was long before you were born," Dante says.

I narrow my eyes. "So why kill Kato now? That was over twenty years ago."

"Think about it. Who would your mother try to contact if she couldn't send word to you?"

My mother is a fighter despite her condition. If she couldn't get through to me…

I let out a breath. "She would contact her family."

I still haven't decided if Kato can be trusted. There's a certain obligation he has to Rebecca since her family are associated with the Triads. But there's a chance he may not believe that my father wants him gone.

He and my father have been in business together for a long time. Kato sends illegal weapons to countries at war, and Adrien's influence with government officials and private ports makes sure they don't run into any trouble with transport. My father needs Kato's money. And Kato's reliance on Harper-Black Industries puts him firmly in my father's pocket like the rest of us, even more so now if what Dante is telling me is true about him and my mother.

My only hope is that he helps me find Rebecca. Then I can finally kill my bastard father without a second thought. But hope is fragile, and this game of cat and mouse is extreme. *Why can't I just kill the bad guys and bathe in their blood? That's all I want to do. Why is that so fucking hard?*

Kato's private quarters are as you'd expect—opulent, overbearing, and full of black and gold. Kato himself is lazing on a love seat in the middle of the room when I enter, dressed in a silver shirt that burns my retinas just to look at it.

Tall, with black hair styled to a side parting, almond shaped eyes—the man is a mix of Asian and English heritage like me. He looks younger than he is. He's my mother's age. They grew up together. But he doesn't have any wrinkles. The only mar on his smooth Asian skin is the scar that runs over one eye and down to his chin. I haven't seen Kato since I was a kid, but I know it's him. Just like he knows who I am now that I'm back in my father's world.

I've heard the stories. I know how he got his scars.

They're the horror stories your parents tell you, so you don't fall out of line.

The maître d takes his leave. Kato smirks and gestures to a matching sofa opposite. I take a seat and stare at him in a way that would unnerve most men.

His grin doesn't falter. "Miss Harper-Black. I heard you were back. I also heard a lot of bad things about you. Tell me…" He takes a swig of his drink, a dark amber-colored liquid. "Are they true?"

I tilt my head. "What do you think?"

He sneers. "I think that you're a spoiled, stuck-up princess like you've always been, and the rumors are just lies spread by your daddy to keep his enemies away from you."

"If you think that then you don't know my father at all," I say, a smile curling onto my glossy lips. "Or me, for that matter."

"Oh, but I do," he says cryptically, a cruel smile on his lips. "Only too well." He leans forward and pours himself another drink. As he shifts, I notice he has a gun under his shirt. One within easy reach. He offers me a glass of the same amber liquid, but I don't take it.

"Did you and my mother fuck?" I ask bluntly.

He chuckles and takes a long swig. "You don't beat around the bush, do you?"

I shake my head. "Life's too short."

"Life's too short, indeed." He nods. "Your mother is an exceptional woman."

I note his use of the present tense in that sentence. Adrien told everyone my mother died when we escaped. There was even a funeral.

Fuck. He knows. Dante was right.

Someone steps from the shadows. It's the maître d. I don't fail to notice his hands covered in blood as he wipes them clean with a cloth.

"What are you…" I start.

"We had a little problem. You were being tailed."

Lorcan. Or Dante?

"Whose blood is that?" I ask, getting to my feet, a spike in adrenaline flooding my veins.

"Some low-down fucker working for your father," says Kato. "Don't worry. He won't be running back to Daddy to tell tales." He indicates for me to sit. "Now, where were we? You were about to offer me a deal in return for not killing me? Have I got that right?"

FIVE

VIOLA

DANTE IS where I left him, outside in the parking lot waiting for me to fuck things up and come to my rescue. I yank open the car door and slide into the seat of his brown Mustang before slamming the door shut.

"What did this car ever do to you?" he says nonchalantly.

"It's brown," I say in a flat response.

He shakes his head. "How did it go with Kato?"

"He's in. He thinks he knows where she is but can't get to her. He's not telling us until he's safely away, but he's agreed to keep Rebecca's family safe from Adrien while we take him out." I look at Dante with a little more intensity. "He's afraid you'll kill him after we get Rebecca back," I say.

"He's right to be cautious."

"And someone knew we were here," I add, looking over at Dante to judge his reaction. My skirt has ridden up, so I purposely leave it and rest one hand on the hilt of my knife which is strapped to my thigh. If this is another one of Adrien's tests, then I've failed massively, and Dante is not someone I should be trapped in a car with.

Dante's gaze sweeps over my legs straight to the blade. He doesn't even blink at seeing my silk panties. I reckon he's dead inside. Someone damaged him as a kid, because there's no heat whatsoever in the way he looks at me.

"Are you planning on using that here?" he says after a pause.

He's got a point. We're in public outside the main entrance of the casino, parked up where the valets and bell boys for the casino pass by often. They keep giving his shitty car looks of distaste. I don't blame them. I wholeheartedly agree this car is an eyesore. Still, it works both ways. Here I'm visible. Safe.

"Not unless I have to," I say sweetly. "Now, where were we?" I say, mimicking Kato's words from earlier. "How did Adrien know we were here?"

Dante sighs. "You think I told him?"

"Who else," I snap. If only Kato's guy hadn't butchered him, I could have tortured the truth out of the fucker. When I said the same to Kato, he just laughed and said it didn't matter. It matters. I can't work like this—in the dark.

"It wasn't me." Dante shrugs, like it's no big deal. It does make more sense than some elaborate mind game that my father and Dante are fucking me over with.

"Then who else? Why would one of Adrien's men be here? Don't you think it's a coincidence?"

"No. Adrien's men usually come here to play cards." He looks me dead in the eyes. "V, you need to trust that I wouldn't do anything to hurt Rebecca."

He is right about that. The monster does have a heart.

I breathe out, letting the tension ease off in my body. I keep expecting someone to fuck me over. Why? I was never this paranoid before. Or this alone with no one to really trust.

Maybe that's why I miss the boys?

"Maybe you should sit the next one out? I can talk to Griffin."

I rub the back of my neck while I refocus on that task at hand, and what Dante is saying to me. "No, I'm fine. I'm just jumping at shadows."

He narrows his eyes but gives a nod. Jumping at shadows is our code word for having an off day. That's all this is—an off day. *I don't need Lorcan or Dino, or even Jude for that matter. I need no one.*

"You know, I could ask you the same questions about lover boy showing up?" Dante says.

Lover boy? Ah, he means Lorcan showing up in the casino.

I scowl. "You saw him then."

"Please tell me you didn't invite him here. I thought you were done with all that."

Dante's chastisement grates me more than I care to admit. Ever since I've been back, he's done nothing but make me feel stupid for 'shacking up with a bunch of teenage boys' in the first place.

"I didn't invite him here," I say, as a loud-as-fuck, canary yellow McLaren screams into the courtyard in front of the casino. A valet gets out and hands the keys to a drunk guy with a giggling blonde in tow, as they stumble out of the front entrance. "Speak of the Devil," I mumble.

Lorcan, shit-faced and oblivious, heads to the driver seat. He's going to drink and drive. I draw the line at watching him do that. The fucker can burn a thousand ways but he's not wrapping himself around a tree for the second time.

I roll my eyes at Dante as I reach for the door hand to let myself out. "I swear, Lorcan being here is a fucking coincidence."

Dante snorts. "I'll wait while you tie up loose ends." As I get out, he adds. "But I won't wait for long."

Fucker.

Ignoring the cat calls from the street surrounding the casino, I saunter over to the McLaren. I don't know what I'm going to do when I get there so I just let my instincts take over. The blood-red rage that was churning inside my gut this whole fucking time is screaming to be let out.

"Get the fuck out," I say to the blonde. My threat is lost to the fact the door is a gull wing, and the seats are so low down I'd have to crawl on my hands and knees to stab her.

Lorcan fixes an unsteady gaze at me from the driver seat and smirks. "Oh, it's you." He looks away, shaking his head.

"Who the fuck are you?" the blonde hisses. She looks at Lorcan. "Who the fuck is she?"

I cross my arms and wait. After a few seconds, Lorcan drifts his attention back to where I'm standing, waiting.

"If you smash your head in again, Saskia will kill you," I say.

"Saskia can go fuck herself," Lorcan drawls. Unlike Dante, he's very much a horny bastard. His eyes seem to glue themselves to my legs, desire flashing behind them as he takes the length of me in. "But I'll always fuck you, sweetheart."

"Charming," I say. "But I'm still driving you home. You're absolutely wasted."

He glances at the blonde next to him. "Piss off."

Lorcan's date looks absolutely livid. "What did you say?"

"I said, piss off, Harmony. Are you deaf?"

"And how do you expect me to get back all the way to Richmond?"

Lorcan gives Harmony a blank look.

She does what I've been wanting to do all night—she slaps him. The cracking sound rings out loud and clear as his head snaps sideways. I almost want to clap.

"Fucking asshole," she says. I sigh and wait while she scrambles around trying to get out of such a low riding vehicle. She doesn't do it gracefully. She tumbles out on her ass, and no one makes a move to help her.

As soon as she vacates, I gracefully replace her in the leather bucket seat. The doors close of their own accord. Trapping me in with yet another guy I don't trust. The seat is still warm. I glare at Lorcan who glares back. The mark on his cheek is bright red. It suits him.

"What are you doing here?" I say.

"What's it look like? I'm on a fucking bender."

"And the blonde?"

"A friend."

"Some friend." I snort. "You just dumped her on the side of the road in the middle of Soho."

"She wanted to slum it, so I brought her here." He looks at me, slightly more sober than I've seen him all night, chartreuse green eyes seeking me out in the low light. Someone beeps a horn behind us.

"I need to move the car."

"I'll do it," I hiss. "Swap seats."

He sighs but starts climbing into the seat I'm occupying. "You're going to have to help by moving?" he says.

"I meant getting out of the car by the doors," I say as his hand wraps around my waist. The familiar feel of him so close sends electric currents through my body.

"Too late," he breathes into my ear, lifting me up by my butt. Somehow, he's maneuvered himself under me. I'm sitting on his lap, nestled against him so I can feel how hard he is through the thin material of my dress. Even my heart starts racing if its own fucking accord.

Shooting my gaze heavenward, I wriggle toward the driver's seat.

His hands tighten, not letting me go. "Not so fast, sweetheart," he drawls

I close my eyes. His woodsy cologne on its own does things to my body without permission, never mind anything else.

I forgot that when I'm with Lorcan, I'm on goddamn fire.

SIX

VIOLA

NO, not happening.

I shove my raging hormones aside and elbow him in the gut. He releases me at once, gasping, and I use the clear way to ease into the driver's seat, as his sharp intake of breath turns to a groan. I, of course, rub myself over his erection without batting an eyelid.

"Viola, you're killing me," he says.

"Good," I say, glancing in the mirror to see if Dante is still parked where I left him. He is. I flash the hazard lights on and off and then pull away. The brown Mustang peels after us, following as I glide the McLaren into London night traffic.

"Where are you staying? The frat house?" I ask him.

"Wherever, I don't care." Lorcan notices me looking in the rearview mirror and clocks the Mustang a few cars back. "Are you going to tell me what you and the psycho were doing at White Jade Casino?"

"No." I glance over at him. His eyes are focused now, alert. He's sobering up. From what I remember of Lor, it doesn't take much to make him clear headed again. We used to go at it all night, like fucking rabbits.

"Always keeping secrets," he sneers, leaning back into his seat with a shake of his head. "I don't miss that about you."

"You don't miss anything about me. Your 'friend' was hanging off your dick at the bar."

His lips curl up and his eyes are practically glowing. He doesn't look upset that I caught him out. "Oh shit, you got me." He holds up his hands.

"You didn't wait long," I say, unable to help myself.

"Ah ah, no you don't. You left us, sweetheart. Not the other way around."

He's right. I told him and Dino to fucking leave me alone the last time I saw them. So why do I feel like driving back to soho and punching that fucking blonde bitch in the face.

"You're cute when you're jealous," he says in a low voice. I'm not ready for his hand on my thigh, making the longing inside my loins harder to bear. Screw the blonde. I want to fuck her out of him.

It's impossible to drive with his fingers teasing up my thigh every once in a while, caressing the silk between my legs.

"Jesus, Viola. You're desperate for me, aren't you? You're soaking."

"Don't you fucking dare," I warn him.

He ignores me, like I knew he would, and unbuckles his seat belt to lean over, bunching my skirt up until I'm exposed to him. "Open your legs, sweetheart," he orders.

"No, I'm driving," I say, using every muscle in my body to keep them shut.

"Stop fighting me. You're ruining my fucking leather." He pushes them apart easily, and then kisses the insides of my thighs. So much for early morning gym sessions with Dante these past couple of months.

"You're a dickhead, you know that?"

"Oh, I know," he mutters before burying his head between my

legs. His tongue is soft velvet as it delves into my folds. I gnaw the inside of my cheek. The taste of blood helps me concentrate on the fucking road because if I'm not careful, we're going to land in a bloody hedge.

I wait until we're on a darkened road, and then pull over. I let go of the wheel, grabbing handfuls of his hair. I'm torn between dragging him off me or riding the building orgasm out. Dante is still behind us in his car. Headlights flash a couple of times as if to say 'why the fuck have we stopped'. I never carry my phone anymore since Adrien confiscated it and then gave it back a few days later with a goddam tracker in it, so Dante can't call me. Any minute he's going to come over to the car to see what I'm playing at.

I say as much. At least I think I'm speaking out loud. The Devil in-between my legs chuckles as I let out a little moan. *Fuck.* This is not what I need. It's the last thing.

It's a good thing I'm not wearing an earpiece.

Lorcan pulls back, in his hands is the knife I keep strapped to my thigh. "Turn around, face the door," he says with a smirk, teasing the blade over my skin. Dante's headlights are still on. If I do, there's a good chance he will see me.

"I'm not letting you fuck me in the car while Dante is parked right behind us."

"Sweetheart, do as I say, or I'll slice this dress clean off."

He fucking would as well. I throw Lorcan a side-eye before unbuckling and pulling my knees up onto the seat.

"Hands behind your back."

Grimacing, I do as he says, resting my head against the cool glass of the window. The sound of the seatbelt unraveling, and the sensation of the thick material around my wrists pulling taut as he knots it, has my heart speeding up and my legs trembling. He uses the blade to nick both sides of my silk panties and runs the steel dangerously close, over my thighs.

Then I feel the hilt at my entrance.

And I'm soaking wet.

My breath catches. This is not what I signed up for. "I thought you were going to fuck me," I scowl.

He yanks the seat belt and my wrists with it, until I'm upright on my knees, head resting back on his chest.

"I don't fuck exes. I just make them suffer for my enjoyment," he drawls. "And I'm going to enjoy watching you come all over this fucking dagger, sweetheart."

Lorcan rams the metal hilt up inside me. I'm not ready for it, but I moan loudly enough anyway. Then he fucks me with the handle of my own blade, while I pant and lean back into him. I'm so riled up, I bite his arm hard. He hisses but keeps up the rhythm. The hilt is warm now and I imagine it's Lorcan's cock inside me, harder than steel, tearing up my insides.

I'm going to feel this tomorrow.

I open my mouth to cry out, but Lorcan seals my mouth with his. His hand moves around the front of my dress and then under it, fingers finding my clit as he rubs it swollen. Every nerve is on fire. Every part of me drenched in sweat.

"You're so fucking wet, every inch of this blade is covered in you," he breathes. "Come for me. And when you use this knife, I want you to think of this fucking moment."

His fingers pinch my clit as he shoves the hilt in as far as it goes.

And sweet release comes all too soon.

"That's it, sweetheart," he says, his voice as smooth as silk. His arm curls around my neck, holding me upright while I quiver hard. All thoughts of Dante possibly watching through the rear window have gone out of my mind.

Or have they?

The bliss afterward is short-lived. I need more.

Without him holding my restraints, I'm able to slip a hand free. I twist and grab his dick through his pants, ignoring the knife he still has inside me.

"You better fuck me now," I demand. Then I kiss him. His mouth seals against mine, and I taste myself on him.

"Nah, I don't think I will," he says, shaking his head, pulling away from my lips.

I frown at him and look at him properly. His eyes are full of malice, tearing into me with wrath so potent if I was anyone else, I would choke. This isn't the way we play the game, the one where we both say 'no' but mean fucking 'yes'.

"You're serious," I say, eyes narrowed.

"You broke Sinner's heart. The poor bastard. I don't know what you did to him, but he's fully invested on doing a fucking job you sent him to do."

I frown. "What job?"

"Getting close to Kristian. Jesus, Viola. I said get him on board, not fucking send him into the jaws of hell. Did he tell you what happened to him before you met? That he tried to kill himself because of Kristian. Why the fuck would you ask that of him and then reject him? He's got it into his head that he owes you. That he needs to fully ingratiate himself into his family for you. To get you back."

"He's with Kristian?" Lorcan's words only half make sense. I did ask Dino to do a job for me the last time I saw him, but it was a throwaway comment. "I only said that to him to get him to toughen up. He's in love with me and he can't be. And you know why."

Because I don't belong with them.

Lorcan looks incredulous and then he snorts a laugh, head still shaking. "Just get out of my car, Viola." He extracts the handle of my knife and offers it to me like a parting gift.

"Here, use this if you're still horny," he snorts.

"You're still drunk," I say, eyes slitted at him.

He smirks. "We're close to Richmond. Harmony will be home by now."

I stare at him like I've been burned. Then I coolly take my blade and get out of the car. The handle of my knife is slippery and wet, but it doesn't matter. It's fucking raining outside anyway.

I walk steadily to Dante's car and shut everything down, freezing it all out. Dante. Lorcan. Dino. Even Jude. I don't need any of them. I only need one thing—myself. The rage I felt earlier is nothing but an irritating memory by the time I get to the passenger door of the Mustang. And I'm soaked through to the bone.

Just in time for the McLaren to start up with a growl and fuck off.

My fingers slip over the door handle as I try to open it. In the end, Dante reaches over and opens the door for me. I climb into the warm car, drenching the passenger footwell and seat. The heaters are on, so I move them so that they're pointed my way. I'm a sodden mess, wig plastered to my face, makeup smeared.

"You know, that's not what I meant when I said to tie up loose ends," Dante says as he looks me over.

I blink at him, ignoring the mascara leaking into my eyes and fucking up my contact lenses. "I don't give a fuck. Let's just go. Griffin is probably waiting."

Approaching both of Adrien's business associates on the same night was Dante's idea but one that makes sense. Once Adrien finds out that I didn't kill Kato or that Dante didn't kill Griffin, and they've both gone underground, he's going to suspect something. We need to find Rebecca before he does.

I know I'm pushing my luck. Dante could turn around and make me walk home for being such a bitch. He's done it before. But he takes one last look my way and switches the engine on.

"If you're not up to it, I can speak to Griffin alone," he says.

"You're not getting rid of me that easily. Anyway, if he sees you and only you, Griffin will shoot you dead before you even get in the door." On top of that, I don't trust Dante. Not hurting Rebecca is one thing, but there's nothing to stop him cutting a deal with Griffin that has me dead in the ground by nightfall.

SEVEN

LORCAN

WHAT THE FUCK *was I thinking?* I shouldn't have used her like that. And as much as I enjoyed bringing her down a peg or two, I shouldn't have told her I was going back to Harmony's.

It was a lie.

I was too fucked to drive. As soon as I was out of sight, I pulled into a lay-by and passed the fuck out. I woke up freezing my dick off the next day on a road rammed with rush hour traffic at a standstill. Took me fucking hours to get home.

Not that I got to sleep in my bed. Emergency board meeting at 9 a.m. sharp had me back on the road after a quick shower and change. With my father gone, there's no one to take the reins but me.

I knock back the whiskey in my shot glass. It's my first drink of the day and it won't be my last. I've had a long day at the office.

God, I sound like my fucking father.

I fill my glass again from the bottle on the bar next to me, just as Dino walks into the members club we both belong to. It's been a few weeks since I saw him last. His brother keeps him busy now that he's decided to embrace the family business. Still, we try to catch up once a week.

"Sinner," I raise my glass in a toast. "You're here for once." He's always fucking making me wait, or cancelling on me. Or should I say his brother drives him to. It makes me wonder what the fuck he does for Kristian that he can't take ten minutes to have a drink with me.

Dino scowls, takes off his coat and hands it to the hostess, and then takes a seat at the bar beside me. I indicate to the bartender to bring another glass and then pour him three fingers. "Get that down you," I say.

He waves his hand. "I'm not drinking this early."

"Why the fuck not?"

He sighs. "Kristian needs me for something after this."

I raise a brow. "More for me then," I say, decanting his into mine.

He asks for a water instead, before frowning my way. I don't think I've seen him smile since she left. She's done a number on us alright.

"So, what's this about Viola? What was she doing at the White Jade?" Dino comes right out with it.

I stupidly left Sinner a message when I was fucked out of my head last night. Why I did that, I've no fucking idea. Viola didn't tell me in the end what she was doing there. Only drug dealers and prostitutes frequent that place. I was surprised to see her— absolutely breathtaking in that long black dress. The wig was different but she's always changing her hair and eyes. After all the shit we've been through, I could recognize her anywhere.

I shake my head and knock back the large shot. "Who gives a fuck?"

She chose him.

"She was there with *him*, wasn't she?" Dino says, frown etched on his face.

Dante. That sick fucking psycho.

"His shitty car was tailing us most of the way home."

"Maybe he's keeping her safe?"

I snort a laugh. "You're fucked in the head. She was covered in bruises." It wasn't hard to miss how skinny she looked and how battered her body was. I shouldn't have left her with him. I should have brought her back to the frat house and fucked her senseless. And then devoured her again in the morning. Tied her to the bed if she tried to leave. That would have been a much better way to wake up. Having her clenched around my dick while I rode her hard, eyes rolling back in her head as she came. There's no way she can hide all her secrets from me when I'm balls deep inside her. No fucking way.

She's mine. She belongs to me.

To all of us.

If that's true, why did she choose him?

"I need to move on and forget she ever existed," I say, taking another large swig of my drink.

"We both do, mate," Dino agrees.

But it's easier said than done. Jude is still in juvie because of her. And since Viola took care of Joseph, the police have been sticking their noses in mine and Saskia's business. Forget our alibis. They're not worth a fuck when Scotland Yard is on your case day and night. *Fucking pigs.*

"Fuck it," Dino exhales, grabbing the bottle, pouring out a generous measure for himself. Almost inhaling his drink in one go. *Atta fucking boy.*

"Have you heard from Jude?" He winces as the single malt does its job. "Are we going to get him out?"

"No, it's proving harder than we thought. And he's convinced Byron is in part of the facility he doesn't have access to, so he's not keen on getting out before the end of his sentence," I snort.

"How long is his sentence?"

"Three months. I spoke to his lawyer. He's done two thirds of it already. He's got less than a month left. He should be out for exams," I say.

"Fucking exams," says Dino, squinting at me. "Are you going to take them? Finally fucking graduate?"

"I don't need to, now that I have my inheritance."

"Lucky you," he sighs, taking a pair of dice out of his pocket. He shakes them and rolls. They land on a three and five. "Fuck me. I guess I'm turning up on exam day."

"You still playing that dumb fucking game?" I say, brow raised.

He shrugs. "I only lose if it's an eight."

"Like you only drive your car into a fucking wall if it's an eight?" I ask, reminding him of a time when he was dumb as shit. We never say it for what it is—Dino Vice tried to kill himself. It would embarrass him too much. But I can't let him forget how weak he let himself become. I'm not scraping him off the tarmac again anytime soon. No fucking way.

"The Five want to meet with me," I say to him. I've been waiting for the invitation ever since Joseph died. The Five meet once a month in a location only disclosed days before. I've met each one of The Five on their own terms and I can say that I'm not particularly fond of any of them. Kristian Vice, Dino's brother, being the worst. Albert Marques, Jude's grandfather who is still very much alive. Graham Baron, Finn's uncle. And Royden Earlshore, Carly's father. They all control some part of my grandfather's organization. The same organization my adoptive father, Joseph, was at the helm of before he died, ultimately passing his position onto me.

"They finally contacted you?" Dino asks. "It's been months."

Like me, Dino was also beginning to think they weren't going to accept me. "The card came this morning," I say. I extract a crisp white card embellished with my name on it and hand it to him.

He takes it and studies it, running fingers over the smooth surface, flipping it in his hands.

"Shit, it's at Harper-Black Enterprises?"

"Would you believe that he's one of our main partners? He owns shares in each of our businesses. Apparently, we ran into supply issues a while back and needed his ports and shipping routes to keep up with demand."

"You're fucking joking. Kristian never mentioned that." He hands it back and runs a hand over his head.

"Your brother tell you everything?"

Dino shakes his head. "You got a point. I thought Joseph was grooming you for this shit."

I give a shrug. "Joseph never fucking trusted me. Part of the reason he was cutting me out of the will. Bet the fucker is turning in his grave now that I've got my hands on his empire and all the sick and twisted shit it's built on."

Dino grimaces.

He knows I'm talking about the child prostitution ring that the organization has let run rampant through their fucking city. The one that has become a fucking rite of passage for us all, including Jude's grandfather, who himself sits at the top of this country's bastardized and damn near corrupt justice system. It's how the organization get their main source of income, and how my father maintained control.

"You still planning to destroy it?"

I arch a brow. "Does Finlay shit himself in the woods?"

Joseph's complete fucking twisted empire is mine to burn to the ground. All of it. I knew he ran the ring since I was in it for most of my fucked-up childhood, but I never knew the extent of it and how much he had on people. That black book was just the tip of the iceberg. Celebs, politicians, even fucking judges—all have been clients of his. And rich, well-to-do families who ran into debt and needed the money, sold their kids to pay it off. Want an Ivy League education? Suck dick for a few months and Bob's your perverted fucking uncle.

The only thing stopping me from exposing the whole sick and twisted network, is Saskia. I need to protect her. Every fucking one of us is implicated because we brought in the others to save our own necks. We'll all go down. Of all people, she doesn't deserve that.

But maybe it's time the rest of us did.

"My father has thousands of names in his books. It would take a lifetime to clean up his fucking mess. And someone will put two and two together and murder me in my sleep." I take a swig of my drink. "Taking down the whole network is the only way this ends."

"Taking the network down will mean taking her father down too. If he was greasing palms for Joseph."

Her. He means Viola. "I know," I say.

"And she'll be at Harper-Black Estate."

"I have to go. I have no choice. I'm supposed to be the leader of the fucking organization now," I say, downing another shot and then finishing off the bottle. "I'm the only fucking Duke left."

Although, some might say I'm not a real Duke, since I was adopted.

I need to get the other four to trust me, so I have to attend. And I should respond soon. The rest of The Five aren't known for their patience.

Out of all of them, I only give a fuck about Kristian Vice, Dino's brother. I want him gone. A couple of the others might decide to back me if it means Vice is no longer part of the organization. Marques is a sure bet. With Jude incarcerated, he's going to want retribution. I need Dino on board with this too. Since he went into the family business, running his dead dad's drug empire with his evil brother, I have to know he has my back.

"You know, Kristian is going to make a play for my position," I say to Dino.

"Marques and Earlshore will back you, surely?"

"No they fucking won't, they're scared of *him*. And your brother is a bomb waiting to go off and you know it. Baron too."

"Baron doesn't give a shit about politics. He will back whoever keeps the ring up and running," Dino says in a low voice as his face darkens. He's right. Baron and Vice have also been circle jerking each other for as long as I can fucking remember. If we start a war with one, the other will follow. But I have no beef with the Barons. And I have something on Finn that'll keep Baron on a short leash.

"I don't give two fucks about Baron. He just needs to stay out of my way while *we* deal with Kristian." I emphasize the *we*.

"Are you asking me to kill my own brother?"

I look directly at him. "No. I'll handle that part."

He exhales and shakes his head. "What about Viola?"

I shake my head. "Forget her. She left us. What we need to do is finish what she started. That's what we need to do."

Dino nods his head.

"So, the plan still stands? Even with Viola gone?"

I give him an evil fucking smile in answer.

Without our Angel of Death, I thought we'd fall apart. She was the glue that held us all together. But with her gone, I can finally see what the problem was all along. I was hiding behind her. She took out Joseph for Saskia when it should have been me. I was too arrogant to get my hands dirty, but you can't be in this world and keep them clean.

The hostess brings us our coats. Our ten-minute meeting is up. No rest for the fucking wicked.

"Don't worry about your brother. Do your exams and then leave this shitty town," I say to Dino.

"I'm not leaving," he says, jaw set, eyes hardened.

I look at him and see the damage she did etched clearly into his features. He's going to break again. He's at the edge ready to step off it. Feeling the weight of every other fucking problem bearing down on me, I nod my head.

"Then how about you ditch Kristian and come with me. I'm off to pay Finn a little visit."

Dino frowns. "Why him?"

"He knows when the pre-meeting to the organization's little shindig is going to be held." Finn called me after I sent him a photo of him with some girl, who did not look like she gave any consent whatsoever. He was the one who gave me the heads up about the invite. His uncle is Graham 'Griffin' Baron after all.

Fucking Finn. He's about as useful as a dick flavored lollipop most of the time. I'm impressed he came through, but also wary. His uncle isn't on my favorite persons list. Still, I trust him more than I do Kristian. Having Dino there might just be the support I need. Especially if Viola's there too.

And just maybe he'll see once and for all…

That she's not fucking worth dying for.

EIGHT

VIOLA

SOMETHING OR SOMEONE must have spooked Griffin because he was gone when we got to his three-story town house in Chelsea Square the same night. There was nothing to do but head back and pretend Kato had been dealt with and that Griffin would be next.

Kato agreed to lie low to buy us time until we find Rebecca. And I agreed to let Dante go looking for her, so as not to arouse suspicion. But it's been weeks. Dante has been gone to the fucking wind ever since.

Where are you, Dante?

Have you left me to rot in hell again?

Adrien is back tonight, and I have to face him alone. I don't mind being stuck in the house all day every day when I don't have to deal with him. I can deal with my own monster. But when he's here, there are two monsters and I know which one I'm more fearful of.

I take time dressing before he arrives. It's either that or pace the room like a caged animal. I've taken to wearing long flowing dresses that show off enough skin to piss him off, and yet hide the ugly scar on my thigh. I don't want to give him the satisfaction of seeing it on my flesh. He doesn't get to see that.

I pick out a red number to match the mood I'm in. I've started dreaming of being covered in blood again. Night after night, Dante comes to me in my sleep and slashes my throat while Lorcan, Jude and Dino watch. Only, in my dreams I'm wearing white.

It's a fucked-up dream but it doesn't take a psychiatrist to work out what the fuck my subconscious feels guilty for.

I'm missing the boys. I didn't think I would. I never miss anyone. But they creep into my thoughts when I'm not expecting it.

The door to my room opens just as I'm fixing my hair. It's Gigi. There are no locks in this house, and Gigi doesn't believe in knocking. She shoots me a toxic look and scowls. She doesn't even need to speak. I know what her being here means. She's never far from Adrien so when she's here, he's near.

"He wants to see me then?"

"Just fucking hurry up," she says, eyes filled with black hate. She didn't like me before, but she absolutely loathes me now. And I know why. After Dante pushed her into the furnace, the fire scarred her hands. She blames me. What irks her more is that my father won't let her touch a hair on my head.

Not that I can't handle her myself.

I follow Gigi downstairs, past the grand hallway, and into the dining room. She pays me no attention as I follow her, but I study her as we walk. I note that she's wearing gloves. Just like me, she's hiding her new scars. I also see where she keeps her set of keys for the house. I said there are no locks in the house, but there are other doors that have them—all the rooms my father doesn't want me in.

"There you are," says Adrien as we enter the dining room. "Viola, it's time you met my business associates." I almost hesitate when I see who the guests are. Gigi is positively full of glee as she seats me next to my father, opposite Graham 'Griffin' Baron and Kristian Vice.

Adrien introduces them both as though I've no fucking idea who they are. Best to play dumb. Adrien thinks all women are idiots, so it's easy to fake.

Of all the fucking people to turn up.

On the far side of the table are three empty seats.

"Are we having more guests?"

"They will be joining us later," Adrien assures as dinner is served. "I thought dinner would be more intimate this way." Intimate indeed. The two people I've been wanting to be in the same room with—one to kill and one to recruit—have been handed to me on a plate.

Kristian flashes an evil grin at me. I've never met him, but I know who is because he looks exactly like an older, more serious version of Dino. Turquoise blue eyes, red hair, but there's a faint silvery scar down one side of his face and hands are covered in rings. There's definitely no dimple in his cheek.

He chuckles, licking his lips as he catches me studying him. "I've heard so much about you," he says.

Griffin on the other hand is old enough to be my father. Dirty blonde hair, lightened with grey, dark brown eyes over a hooked nose. Again, I've never met him, but I know who he is. He's well known in hitman circles for being a steady source of work. I just never linked him to my father until Dante showed me the files.

Griffin studies me just as intently as I study him, then he focuses on Adrien.

"Why am I here, Adrien? If you're going to cut me loose do it fucking soon because I don't have time for your bullshit."

Kristian sniggers and I raise a brow and wait for Adrien's reaction. Interesting. Griffin has balls after all. After he fled, I was beginning to think him a coward. But if he was, there's no way he'd come into the lion's den as alone as he is now.

Adrien smirks. "Straight to the point, Grif, as always. That's what I've always liked about you. You're here because with Ethan gone it's time I got a new second-in-command."

I shoot a glance at my father. I assumed he was going to promote Kristian. Not that I care. What he does is of no interest to me unless it has something to do with Rebecca. The buzzing under my skin itches to leave this damn place and go and find her myself. But Adrien won't like me leaving. I'm not allowed to unless he gives consent. If I don't play the good daughter—kill or fuck who he tells me to, the way he tells me to—Rebecca dies.

"And that's me right, HB? I'm the one who's been fucking loyal all these years," snipes Kristian.

"I don't give a fuck who you make your second," Griffin says. "I came here to talk about dividing Kato's business now he's gone."

"Kato's guns and contacts will go to who I fucking say so," says my father acidly. His eyes are glacial. I know Adrien. He probably has a gun under the table. "And that will be my second in command."

Kristian smirks, looking triumphant.

Griffin glares at Adrien. "The others won't like it."

"Screw the fucking organization. Duke is gone," Kristian sighs. "It's a fucking free for all now and you know it."

Like a slot of the puzzle clicking into place, I'm suddenly aware that killing Joseph has opened up Pandora's box.

I whip my head to my father.

Did he orchestrate this whole fucking thing? Have I been a pawn this whole time?

Mouth dry, I stare at him until he flicks a gaze my way. The knowing way he looks at me spikes rage through my body until I can't stop trembling. I'm not listening to the conversation until Griffin scowls and Kristian looks practically livid, burning a hateful gaze right at me.

"You're fucking joking," Kristian spouts. "She's your fucking second?"

'Interesting move," Griffin says, watching me warily now.

I'm still shaking so I force myself to stop.

"Are you cold?" Griffin asks. "Or absolutely terrified?" I'm neither cold, nor scared. It's the rage that consumes me. I don't bother to correct him. I run the last few moments back in my head. Adrien just announced me as his fucking second.

"She's a fucking mess, if you ask me. Look at her."

"Is that right?" Adrien warns in a dangerously calm voice. Gigi and another of Adrien's security guards step forward, aiming their guns at Kristian's and Griffin's head as he speaks.

Both men also reach for their guns but it's too late. The stalemate is set. Griffin doesn't move but he looks unimpressed. Kristian's eyes blaze with contempt and burning rage.

"Are you cold or terrified, my dear?" my fathers asks.

I glare at Adrien.

"Cold," I say because telling Adrien the truth will backfire. Emotion is a weakness.

"Of course you're cold. You're wearing hardly anything." He looks at Kristian. "Give her your jacket."

Kristian stares at my father like he's sprouted wings. He growls as he gets to his feet, slips off his tailored jacket, and tosses it to me.

I calmly drape it over my shoulders. It's warm and smells of Kristian's cologne. Annoyingly, It's the same one Dino wears and it makes my chest tighten. I suck in a breath, soothing my raw edges with a sip of wine. At that moment, the staff appear and serve us the first course.

Adrien sighs and waves his men away. Gigi, still glaring, puts away her gun. The rest follow.

Adrien looks about the table, elbow resting on it with fingers interlaced. "My daughter is the obvious choice, of course. She is my only heir. Now, let's enjoy our meal before we talk business again," he says, trying to smooth things over. No one is happy but we can at least all eat now that the food is here.

It's foie gras, Adrien's favorite. I stare at it and then ignore it.

As the plates are put in front of each person, no one but my father dives in straightaway to eat.

Kristin huffs and picks at his plate, keeping his eyes on me the whole time. He's looking at me like he wants to skin me alive. That's fine. The feeling is mutual. Griffin is also looking at me, but not with hatred. He's assessing me. Adrien has a reputation and Griffin is trying to figure out the angle.

It's amusing to watch because they have no idea. Men always underestimate me. That's the angle my father is using here.

He's always using me.

Everything I've done in my life is because Adrien was pulling the strings. He always has been…

"It's been a long time, daughter. I was beginning to think you'd never come back for your legacy."

"Legacy?" I snort.

"All of this. It's yours, you know."

I look around. "Why would I want a dump like this?"

"Maybe not the house, but the money, the assets. Your inheritance."

"I don't want any of it."

"Oh, but you will. And there are men that would die to have you along with it."

"We were never yours," I say. A futile remark. He's not even listening.

"When you ran away, I knew where you'd gone. Dante watched over you for me. Kept you from harm. You needed to leave the nest to grow, but now it's time for you to come back. Take your place with me in our empire."

"Fuck the empire," I say with a smile.

"What I want to know," says Kristian, picking a grape from his plate and peeling it. "Is why you've kept this delightful creature hidden all these years. If she's your heir, why have you not let her out to play until now?"

Adrien nods, wiping his mouth after finishing his food. "She was in training."

Training. The care home I was beaten at. The foster home that abused me. Dante. Polina. Even the boys. I've no idea what's real or what was designed by my father to make me what I am now.

Maybe my father knew where Rebecca was all along.

Dogs bark in the distance, so I know someone has arrived. They're the same dogs trained to rip me to pieces should I try to run. Killing them would be the simple option but just like children, I can't bring myself to lift a finger towards animals.

I would rather let the dogs eat me.

The next course is venison. Another of my father's favorite dishes. I can't bring myself to taste the meat, so I ignore the plate in front of me while the men dig in.

The door to the dining room opens. My heart almost stops fucking beating when I see who it is.

Dino Vice.

Lorcan Duke.

And Finlay Baron.

Like one big fucking happy family.

NINE

DINO

WHY IS *she wearing Kristian's fucking jacket?*

That's all I can think about as we enter the room where Viola is sitting, eating dinner with her father, Kristian, and Griffin like it's the most civilized thing to do in the world. This is the second time I've been here and both times I've wanted to tear this place apart to bring Viola home. She doesn't belong here.

Not with Adrien Harper-Black.

And certainly not with fucking Kristian.

My brother may be surprised to see me, but he won't let any weakness show. Instead, he gives me a sly grin. "Baby brother, you made it," the fucker says, putting down his fork. It's all for show. He had no idea I was coming.

"Ah, Duke, you're here. Who have you brought with you?"

"Finlay Baron and Kardinal Vice," Lorcan says smoothly. "They're here to witness any negotiations."

He looks at us and nods. "Fine. We can add more seats," says Adrien.

The staff bustle in with more chairs and place settings and the three of us join the table. There's an awkward fucking moment when no one speaks, but then Viola rolls her eyes. "Excuse me, I need to go to the ladies room."

She dumps the jacket off and stalks out. Every single male in the room watches her go, even my fucking brother. I'm itching to follow her. The last time we spoke she said things that had to be lies. She said it to hurt me. To make me leave. I know she did. And like a twat, I listened and left. Viola's been hurt all her damn life and there I go, adding to the pain. I should have refused to go. I should have shown her that she has me. If no one else, she'll always have me.

Fuck it.

I get up from the table and all eyes look to me. "I need to go to the bathroom," I say. When no one says anything, I walk in the direction Viola disappeared with the intent to find her.

She's standing against the wall with her eyes closed when I enter the bathroom. It wasn't locked. I close it shut behind me and realize there isn't one, so anyone could just walk in. I must be standing there for too long staring at the door handle because she speaks first.

"It doesn't lock," she says.

"I can see that," I sigh, leaving the door closed over instead, walking over to where she's standing.

Her hair is pinned up, piled on top of her head to show off her elegant neck and the jewelry adorning her throat and ears. Dressed in red, she looks absolutely stunning. Just how I remember her.

I stand in front of her, hands in pockets, while she breathes in and out like she's trying to calm herself down.

"Why are you here?" she says eventually, opening her eyes. "I meant it when I said for you all to leave me alone."

I give her a look that borders on hate, because I still don't know how my shitty heart feels toward her anymore. The love is still there, but she tore it apart the day she told me she didn't love me. Every time I breathe in, it hurts. Every time I swallow, it fucking hurts.

"I didn't come for you. I came for Lor. He's a member of The Five now. The others are turning up later in the day. They're having some kind of annual general meeting here," I say eventually, meeting her eyes.

"Lorcan is a member now because Joseph is dead?"

"He's the last surviving male Duke heir, unless you count Byron, his cousin, who no-one knows is still alive."

"I thought Byron was a Marques?"

"Technically, he's also a Duke on his mother's side."

She tosses her head. "It's all a bit fucking incestuous, if you ask me." Her eyes bore into me, burning away what's left of my resolve. "So, you're here to witness the carnage, are you?"

"Something like that." I shake my head. "Look, it doesn't have to be like this. If you came home—"

"Home." She snorts, pushing her body away from the wall she was leaning on. "I told you I'm already home. This is where I belong."

As she starts to walk out, I seize her by her wrist and haul her toward me. Hard enough to make her glare. But she lets me manhandle her. Like me, sometimes she only understands pain. "Just tell me what's in it for you? Staying here with him. Playing at being someone I know you're not. There must be a reason," I say, looking down at her. Her body in that glorious fucking red dress is pressed against mine. I'm hard in an instant.

"Nothing you need to get involved in," she says, looking up at me from under her lashes. But she doesn't make a move to pull away. Alone, she's less defensive. Finally, putting her guard down.

"See, that's where you're wrong. You should involve me..." I say softly. My arm automatically cradles her waist, my fingers stroking the small of her back where the dress is cut out. "...In everything."

She sighs audibly, relaxing into my embrace. "Why do you boys make this so damn hard? Hmmm."

Fuck. I can't leave her here.

Not after this.

Lorcan is going to throttle me.

"I told you. I'm never leaving you."

She trembles in my arms.

"Are you cold?"

She gives a harsh laugh. "No, I'm fucking livid. You never listen to me. But I need you fucking to. I need to go back to the table." This time she tries to push me off her.

"Not yet." I keep her firmly in my arms. She's so petite, it's easy to do. I could easily sling her over my shoulder and walk out of here. She'd probably cut my balls off for doing so, but I could.

She looks up at me again and I can't fucking help it. I have to kiss her. Her lips are sweet and soft. She doesn't pull back, instead she sighs again and melts into me. Drunk on the taste of her, I shove her lightly against the bathroom wall. I want to rip that dress off her and worship every part of her gorgeous body. I want to ease my hard cock inside her and fuck her for hours and hours.

She bites my tongue.

A moan escapes her as my hand slips beneath her dress and I stroke the soft slip of silk between her legs.

She's soaking wet.

Fuck dinner. I'm taking her right here, right now.

I tease her panties aside and delve into her folds with my fingers. Ever since she fucked Lor right in front of me, I've been dreaming of this—taking what's mine.

The bathroom door opens. I break away, turning to see who the fuck it is.

It's Kristian.

"Baby brother, not saving any fucking dessert for the rest of us?"

"Fuck off, Kris. Can't you see we're busy?" I snap.

"You're with the wrong brother you know," he says to her.

"I think I'm with the brother who knows how to handle a woman," Viola retorts.

"If you like dickless. Did he tell you he pissed his fucking pants instead of pulling the fucking trigger the other day? Baby brother doesn't have the balls to show a woman like you a good time."

He's talking about the prostitute I refused to execute because she accidentally scraped his cock with her teeth when he shoved it too far down her throat. I stare at him, jaw clenched.

"Anyway." He saunters into the bathroom and starts unzipping his trousers to take a piss. The room is large for a downstairs restroom, but not spacious enough that I'm comfortable with him taking a fucking piss right there.

He sighs as he empties his bladder and looks over his shoulder. "Oh, don't mind me. Carry on."

Viola, visibly shaking again, takes my hand and digs her nails in so hard I'm pretty sure she's drawn blood.

I let her. If that's what she needs.

"We should go back to dinner," she says nonchalantly. Outwardly, she appears calm. Only I can feel her body practically vibrating, being as close as I am. If she was livid before, she's probably seething now.

As am I.

Fucking Kristian.

"You should, we missed you." He grins at Viola, shakes off and then tucks himself back into his trousers. "We've solved your father's one true heir problem.

Viola's whole body stills as I hold her. "What do you mean?"

"Oh, where's the fun in me telling you without an audience? Why don't you run back to your father and ask him?"

She blinks at him and then pulls away from me. "I don't fucking have time for this," she says, walking off.

My brother smirks. "Kards," he says, using my nickname from when we were kids. "I never knew you had it in you. I assumed she was a frigid little bitch."

"Go anywhere near her, Kristian…"

He walks up close, still fucking smiling like he knows a secret he'll never tell. "Or you'll what? What will you do, little brother?"

"I'll kill you," I say softly. And I mean it.

His smile widens, eyes glazing over making him look insane. "Ah. There's the Kardinal I know and love, right fucking there. Who knew the little bitch was all you needed to grow a pair of balls? Can't wait to see what you do when I slice her to ribbons and fuck every bloody hole I make red fucking raw."

I clench my jaw, fists tightening as he says my worst fear come true. Kristian torturing her. It's his thing. It's what he does. This is why I've kept her from his radar for so long. Once my brother gets excited about someone, he won't stop. The girls he rapes and tortures just for fun never survive. Viola isn't just any girl, but I can't let my brother near her regardless.

She's not as strong as she thinks she is.

He'll destroy her.

TEN

VIOLA

ON THE WAY back to the dinner table, I make a stop to my bedroom. On top of the door frame there's a loose piece of wood. I jig it back now and retrieve my phone. I've gotten used to not having my phone on me at all times, and keeping it hidden so it can't be used against me. But there are times when just sitting around waiting doesn't quite cut it.

I need Dante.

This dinner is turning out to be a fucking nightmare.

I bypass the usual messenger app since I know my father has those tracked, and log into the secure vault Quinn and I used to use to communicate. There are a few new documents in there since I last checked. None from Dante especially. I create a new one titled 'D' and add a message, hoping that when he logs in, he'll see it.

Where are you? I need you back here right now.

I don't wait for a reply. Instead, I put the device back in its hiding place and replace the piece of wood. He'll reply when he has a moment to, or he won't. Either way, he knows I need him here.

When I get back to the dining room, Kristian and Dino are already back in their seats. Kristian's eyes are shining brighter than before, as he stares at me intently from the moment I enter. *He must have taken something. He's completely off his face.*

Dino on the other hand.

He's looking at me like I'm the light of his life. I let my guard down when he kissed me, and he knew it. He's always been the one to break down my barriers. Jude just plows through them and Lorcan waits patiently like a cat waiting for a mouse. But Dino is a coaxer. He knows just what to say to get me to open up.

I head to my own seat, glancing around the room as I do.

Griffin and my father are in deep discussion. Finn is smirking at me, looking me up and down in a feral kind of way. And Lorcan is just watching. His eyes are a dark forest green, shuttered and emotionless. Unlike Dino who wears his heart on his sleeve, I have no idea what Lorcan is thinking or feeling just by looking at him.

But I have a gut feeling he's still angry with me. I've lived with him for long enough to be able to judge his mood. When he closes himself off like this, he's annoyed.

"You're back," Adrien says, looking up. He nods at Gigi who comes over to where I'm sitting and puts her hand on the back of my chair.

"Sorry, women's issues. Did I miss anything?"

Kristian snorts. "Only the main course. You missed the whole fucking thing, love. Oh, and your father just offered you to the highest bidder."

I was waiting for this. Adrien announcing me as his second would come with a fucking price. I'm not dumb enough to think he rates women any higher than he did when I was born. The only reason he's even entertaining me right now is because I bear his name. Once he sells me, he'll have his much-coveted son-in-law, and I'll be another fucking Rebecca. Another trophy that spits out an heir when needed.

Calmly, I take my steak knife and slice the bloody slab of meat on my plate into a small enough portion to eat. Then I proceed to devour my dinner. I'm starving. Once I've finished, and I've dabbed my mouth with my napkin, I turn my attention back to the room, secretly stashing the steak knife under my skirt.

There's a silence mounting as no one says anything. Dino is watching Gigi like a hawk and Lorcan is frowning.

I'm ready for her when she wraps an arm around my upper half and tries to hold me down. Dino jumps to his feet and so does Lorcan, but Adrien calmly takes a gun from its hiding place under the table and points it at me. "Unless you all sit back down, she's dead."

Reluctantly they all sit down. Dino looks worried. Lorcan's expression hasn't changed but there's a tightening to his jaw that wasn't there before. Kristian drapes his arm around his brother, a dark grin plastered onto his face.

I'll give them points for trying.

But I'll get out of this myself.

Adrenaline surges as I stab Gigi in the thigh. She grunts, managing to keep her arm locked over me. I jerk back, smashing my skull into her nose instead. The crack is loud and she loosens her grip.

"Fucking bitch," she snarls.

I don't bother wasting my breath in a retort.

I twist my body and wrench the knife out of her leg, only to ram it in again. She crashes to the floor, taking me and the chair with her. Adrien's men appear as I get to my feet and restrain me, while Gigi, red-faced, bleeding fast, gets up and limps over to us. She grabs a fist full of my hair.

Another one of Adrien's men approaches with what looks like a tracking anklet, similar to the ones used for prisoners on parole. I kick at him but he seizes my leg. I can feel Gigi's nails digging in my scalp as she yanks my head back hard enough to make it fucking hurt. I refuse to scream but I do stop moving. It's taken three of them to hold me. I know when I'm completely over-powered.

Everyone in the room watches in morbid fascination as he places it tightly around my ankle. There's a beeping sounds as he activates the lock.

"What are you doing to her?" exclaims Dino, probably dying inside that he can't save me this time.

Adrien gives him a bank look. "Making sure my asset is well-protected."

Dino shakes his brother off. "What is that?" he spits out. "What the fuck does it do?"

Kristian chuckles. "Calm down, little brother, it's just a tracker."

Gigi lets go of me, and so do the others. I pick myself up with a grimace and glare at my father. When I was a kid, I learned how to get out of the ankle bracelets. But this one is a model I've never seen. Adrien has moved on since I was twelve, obviously.

Adrien looks at me. "If you are quite finished, take your seat."

When I don't move, Adrien moves his hand holding the gun until it points at Dino. "Now."

Kristian's face darkens but my father doesn't notice.

Interesting. He doesn't like that.

I brush myself off, suppressing the burn inside my chest at my father for threatening what's mine, and take my place at the table.

But Adrien keeps the gun on Dino.

I look around. The steak knife is gone. Gigi must have picked it up.

"So, whose offers are on the table already?" I ask sweetly, gritting my teeth. Adrien nods, taking my interest as further evidence of my newfound obedience.

I can feel the tracking device weighing my foot down as I cross my legs.

"Mine, of course," says Kristian, practically licking his lips.

"And mine," Dino pipes up.

Lorcan looks at me darkly but doesn't utter a fucking word. Finn laughs when no one else offers.

"Fuck it, I'll put my hat in the ring," says Griffin gruffly.

I arch a brow. Griffin is twice my age and then some. Still, he's good looking for an older man. I wouldn't say no, but I'm surprised. He has daughters my age already from his previous marriage. And the way he looks at me isn't the same way the others do.

"If we're all doing it, then count me in too," says Finn, still chuckling.

I roll my eyes.

I refuse to look at Lorcan who hasn't even deigned to speak to me since he arrived. As the staff appear to take away the dinner plates and bring dessert, there's movement at the corner of my eye from Lorcan's seat.

"Well, I'm not. I'm fucking done for the night," Lorcan clips out, throwing his napkin on the table, stalking out of the room.

Dino openly scowls at the retreating form of his friend. I don't even bother to waste energy on making a facial expression. I expected Lorcan to act like this. It's what he does. He's just like me in that way. Petulant.

"I'll review the offers and make my decision by tomorrow evening. I'm having some friends over. You're all invited to stay, of course. We have plenty of beds," Adrien says. "Now if you'll excuse me, I have more guests to attend."

Dino throws me a look to say, 'we're staying'.

"Wait, do we not get to test the goods?" Kristian says smoothly. I look at him as he regards me back, leaning in his chair like he already owns the estate and everything in it.

Dino's jaw tightens and he shoots a dangerous look at his brother. "What the fuck, Kristian?"

"I'd like to know that answer too," says Finn, smirking.

Adrien's face darkens. "No one is to touch one hair on her head or take my daughter off the premises until I've made my fucking decision. Got that?"

"Of course," Kristian says. "No touching until tomorrow."

As soon as my father leaves, I give Kristian a deadpan look. "Try it any-fucking-time and I'll castrate you."

Kristian flashes an evil grin back, eyes starry like he's discovered his fucking soulmate. "Careful, baby, you'll make me fall in love with that sort of talk."

Dogs bark in the distance again. My father's so-called business partners have arrived. We don't have to wait long for the rest of the organization to turn up.

"Now we're all here, let's get started," says Adrien as he enters, accompanying the remaining two of The Five, Albert Marques and Royden Earlshore, into the dining room.

"Aren't we waiting for Duke?" asks one of them.

"Unfortunately, Duke has chosen to opt out of this one," says Adrien.

Kristian scoffs. "He's a fucking pussy, just like Joseph if you ask me."

"Who are you calling a pussy?" Lorcan drawls, strolling back into the room. His eyes are slightly brighter than usual. I wouldn't put it past him to have taken a little something to take the edge off. I'm tempted to join him. Thankfully, no one seems to have noticed.

Dino looks relieved, quite the opposite to his brother whose expression is one of extreme distaste.

Clearly this isn't over yet.

Not by a long fucking shot.

ELEVEN

VIOLA

AFTER THE MEETING IS OVER, we're excused, and Adrien retires to his quarters. Dino doesn't leave my side the rest of the night. He won't even let me go to my room.

"You don't think that's the first place Kristian will try it on?"

He's convinced Kristian is going to kidnap me. I have my doubts. Kristian isn't stupid and also, I've never needed Dino to stay safe. All I've needed is myself.

And my cunning.

In my bra are the keys I snatched off Gigi when she was wrestling me. I swiped them while I stabbed her. She'll notice soon that they're missing, so we don't have much time. We're in his room, or the room one of the staff led Dino to after he convinced Finn to stay. Finn is most likely in a room not too dissimilar to this one. Lorcan, I've no idea. No one has seen him since he left the dining room a second time.

I refuse to find him and check on him. He can do drugs and drive, or what the fuck he likes. I'm done being his babysitter.

He's probably gone to fuck Harmonica or whatever her name is.

95

Not that I care.

"Come on, let's go," I say, taking Dino by the hand.

"Why? Where are we going?"

"To fulfill a promise," I say. I look back at him. "It's time to fuck the empire."

My father's office is in a separate part of the estate. It's a library slash office in that his desk is at the far end and around it is shelves and shelves of books. Walnut paneling, huge leather seats, and bookcases adorning every wall. There are also filing cabinets filled with untraceable paper. My father's whole life is in here.

I point Dino at one of the cabinets and toss him the key.

"What are we looking for again?"

"Evidence of where Rebecca might be. Kato thinks she's in one of the halfway houses my father owns. He just doesn't know which one." On the way up here, I explained to Dino why I needed to stay. Keeping him in the dark would just make him harder to control, and since he's not going to leave my side all night, I may as well use him.

Adrien funds a charity for runaways, giving girls who have no place to go a home. It makes him appear to be a caring benefactor when the opposite is true. I know for a fact that those homes are rife with sex predators, because that's how I started out—carving up the fuckers who preyed on the vulnerable girls in those homes by pretending to be a runaway myself.

Ironically, I *was* a runaway. Only, I had money and contacts. And Dante.

"And we can't just check all of them?"

"That's what Dante is doing," I say.

Dino frowns as he rifles through a stack of papers. "I don't understand how he's on our side now."

"He's not. Dante is on his own side." Usually the one that pays him the most money but after recent events, I'm not so sure. I close one drawer after finding fuck all, and then open the one below it.

"And you trust him?"

"No, but my mother did." And I did once too. All this questioning is making my head hurt. *Why the hell did I involve Dino again?*

"I still don't fucking understand," Dino says shaking his head.

Inside the drawer I'm looking in are some interesting files. One of them has my name on it, the other has Dante's. Heart erratic in my fucking chest, I take out Dante's and start to read. After a few seconds I stop trying to understand what I'm reading, close the file and look up. Dino is quiet over his side of the office. Maybe he found something too. "Did you find something?" I say.

"I think so. What's this? Didn't you say your mother was at Beckbridge House before your father found her?

He yanks out an official looking set of papers and hands it to me. I skim them quickly, while Dino looks over my shoulder with his hands around my waist. "It's a transfer request from a few months back. It says it was requested that she was moved to a place closer to home."

Who would have the authority to move her? The moment the request came through, I should've been alerted.

I drop my gaze to the requestor and their signature. "Fuck."

"What?"

"It says the request was put in by me."

"Your father could have faked your signature."

"No, it's more than that. They would only have released her to me." I reach into Dino's pocket and take out his phone. Then I snap a photo of the transfer request and Dante's file and slip his phone back into his pocket.

"This was in the same envelope," Dino says, handing me a flash drive. I walk over to my father's laptop, start it up, and then slot it in.

"You know the password?" Dino asks as I unlock it on the first try.

"What do you think I've been doing in this house for the last two months," I say, looking at him.

Dino narrows his eyes at me, and then nods.

The drive only has one file on it. A video. I press play and recognize what it is immediately. It's footage from the security camera behind the front desk of Beckbridge House. A young girl with long blonde hair peeking out from beneath her hoodie comes into reception. She signs something and a moment later they wheel my mother out. The girl, whoever she fucking is, leaves with Rebecca just as a van pulls up outside and three men in dark suits get out. They hoist my mother's wheelchair into the vehicle and leave. Then the tape ends. I rewind it and watch it again, noticing the time stamp is the same date of the transfer request.

"At least now I know it couldn't have been Dante. He excels at so many things but looking like me isn't one of them."

"Could he have hired an actress and the muscle?" Dino says.

Dante works alone. Always alone. Working with me was the exception. No. If Dante wanted to move my mother, he would do it in a way that involved no one else. Fuck pretending, he'd just break in.

I say all of this to Dino who just huffs. "Let's not talk about that fucker anymore," he says. "It's giving me a headache."

That girl wasn't an actress. I know who she is. I also recognized Griffin's men in the video. I don't say that to Dino. I just shrug and take the drive out of the laptop and then shut it down. Then I tuck the drive into my bra, hiding it out of sight as I rearrange my cleavage.

Dino is watching me, moistening his lips.

"Let's go," I say.

"Not just yet," Dino says, tugging me back into his embrace. He kisses my neck and slips a hand inside my bra, squeezing my breast. "You can't flash me like that and then leave me like this." He presses against me so I can feel how hard he is as he teases my nipple.

"Not here," I say, even though a small moan escapes me.

"You weren't complaining in the bathroom," he says in a velvet soft voice.

We're interrupted by the door to the office opening.

It's Kristian leaning against the entrance. "You two seem to be at it like rabbits. Keeping her all to yourself again, little brother, that's hardly fair. Sharing is caring," he says.

Dino pushes me behind him as though to protect me. I roll my eyes. I'm not interested in watching the Vice brothers fight over me.

"Let me handle this," I say to Dino, passing him the papers. "Can you put these back the way they were?"

"Wait," Dino says but I push past him, shooting him a look over my shoulder. "Just listen to me for once." Dino frowns, but then sighs and turns to the cabinet and the mess of paper. Leaving me to deal with his brother blocking the exit.

"Move," I say to Kristian as I reach him.

When he doesn't, I smile sweetly, stalk right up to him, and grab him by the balls. I don't hesitate to dig my nails in. He flinches, but his eyes twinkle and he groans like he's turned on. *Great. Another Vice who likes being tortured. Were they dropped on their heads as children?*

"Move or I'll snap one off," I say, meaning his balls.

"I meant what I said. You're with the wrong brother. I know what you are, and he is nothing like you."

"You're right," I say, twisting harder. "He's nothing like me."

He grins, pressing closer, ignoring the harsh way I'm holding him, wrapping a hand around mine instead to tighten my grip. "You're more like me than you know. Breaking you is going to be sweet fun," he says softly in the shell of my ear.

It's moments like this I wish I had my knife. Narrowing my eyes, I switch tactics and shove my other elbow into his gut. He chokes a laugh, but releases me, stepping back to leave just enough room for me to squeeze through.

We stare at each other in hatred for a few seconds, and then his gaze shifts behind me as Dino approaches. "Kardinal. A word."

Dino gives him a murderous look but then gives Kristian what he wants. He goes outside the office where Kristian is. I stare at them from inside the doorway as they talk in hushed voices. Dino is either a really good actor and is well practiced at pretending to like his brother, or he's never going to betray him.

Whereas, he's betrayed me before.

He drugged me.

I take a breath and shake my head to clear it. Kristian doesn't scare me. Dino double crossing me does.

"I'll see you later, petal," Kristian suddenly says to me, and disappears down the corridor leaving Dino to come back.

"You're not sleeping alone," Dino says, pulling me into his arms.

I flick my eyes heavenward. *Save me from boys who think they are men.*

"I can handle myself," I snort, pushing him away, locking the office and inserting the key in my bra next to the drive. I'm shaking again because the anger is back.

Fuck, I am paranoid. I need to get a grip, or I'll lose it like I did when I attacked Dante. Lorcan's words are the only thing keeping me sane right now, convincing me that Dino isn't the enemy.

"He's got it into his head that he owes you. That he needs to fully ingratiate himself into his family for you. To get you back."

I breathe in and out, and tuck that little concern of mine deep down somewhere I can deal with it later.

Dino's words come back into focus. "Viola, are you listening?"

"What were you saying?"

"I was saying you don't know Kristian. He's messed in the head when it comes to women."

I suck in another breath and let it out. My hand has stopped shaking. "Then let him try it. I'll do what I've been wanting to do since he ran Lorcan off the road," I say testing the waters. *Fuck Dino and his wavering conscious.*

Dino's face hardens. "You're going to kill him?"

"I told you I would."

Dino looks at me like I'm a monster and he's only just realized. "He's my fucking brother," he says after a pause. "Let me do it."

"No." It's me who has to get blood on her hands. Not only do I enjoy it, I crave it. Lorcan was right, Dino shouldn't have to carry that around with him.

If anyone should be paranoid, it should be the boys about me.

They're not the monsters.

I am.

TWELVE

VIOLA

THE NEXT MORNING, I wake up early before it's even light to check my phone for messages. Then I grab some sports gear from my room and go for a run. There's nothing from Dante yet so I can only imagine he was too busy to check in. I use the run to sort through my thoughts.

There's a flare of dawn in the sky as I push my body to the point where I'm gasping for breath. The cold has seeped through my clothes to my skin, chilling the sweat and burning my lungs.

Reminding me…

I'm not dead.

Yet.

I run for a while longer. When I get to the edge of Adrien's property, my anklet starts going berserk. I slow down to a stop, panting, and glance down at it. The light on the side is flashing red.

When I was younger, I watched one of Adrien's whores get dragged back to him with her leg blown off. I always thought at the time that one of the security men might have done it with a shotgun. But now…

Has the fucker really put an exploding fucking leash on me?

"I wouldn't go too far if I were you."

I spin around to see Gigi, face smug. What I wouldn't give to peel that face off, strip by strip. She must see that in my eyes because she steps closer and closer until she's right on top of me. I, on the other hand, have nowhere to go. If I keep moving back who the fuck knows what will happen. I wouldn't put it past Adrien to have collared me in a way that means I physically can't leave. Not if I want to keep my fucking leg.

"Back off, Gigi," I say, looking up at her. She's taller than me. But that just means she underestimates me.

She steps closer again. "If you want to try and escape, I won't stop you. In fact, I may just help you."

The bitch is going to push me.

I brace myself, lowering the center of gravity, knees bent and locked. It's a fighting stance for women that's meant to make it impossible to be moved or tackled to the ground. Quinn was the one who taught it to me when we used to train together.

I don't get to find out if it holds up because the scream of an engine revving makes us both startle.

I glance behind me as Gigi looks over my shoulder.

A disgusting yellow McLaren roars onto the driveway and then pulls up beside us. The window is down enough for Lorcan to stick his head out.

"Get the fuck in."

I don't wait for a second invitation. I walk around Gigi and then step around the front of the car. I slide into the soft leather bucket seat, and as I pop the seatbelt closed the car takes off toward the estate.

"You went home?" I say as we pull into the courtyard in front of the house.

"I wasn't fucking staying here all night. I almost didn't come back." Of course he didn't. Lorcan needs someone to hold him or he can't fucking sleep. I haven't forgotten.

"Harmonica kicked you out early?"

Lorcan snorts. "As a matter of fact, the other way around."

"Good for you," I say. Then after a moment I add "You shouldn't have come back."

"I keep my promises. Unlike some."

I wrack my brain to think of a promise to him that I've not fulfilled yet. "I told you. I'm working on killing Kristian," I say.

"No, you sent Dino to keep tabs on him while you played happy fucking families with your stepbrother."

So that's it. He's jealous.

"I never told you Dante was my stepbrother."

"It was easy to find out once I knew your last name. Just tell me you're not fucking related, and I'll walk away. I won't bother you anymore. He can have you. You both fucking deserve each other." It doesn't take a well-trained assassin to see the fear in him. It's in the way he grips the steering wheel, the way he clenches his jaw and keeps his eyes narrowed and staring straight ahead.

I cock my head. *If I say we're not related and that there's nothing going on, will he believe me?* My mind flits back to the file I found on Dante in Adrien's study. Dante must not know what's in that file. But now is not the time to unpick dark secrets. I'll deal with that later.

I turn my attention to Lorcan who is staring at me with dark eyes filled with pain. "Adrien isn't his real father and his mother is dead."

"So, you're fucking him then?" he asks.

"No," I say.

"But you want to."

There's a longing inside me that wants to lie down and have Lorcan wrap his arms around me like he used to when he'd sneak into my room late at night. Those are the moments I miss.

Weak moments.

Out of control ones.

Ones where I share secrets that aren't mine to tell.

I'm better off alone.

In answer to his question, I get out of the car.

"Fucking coward," he says under his breath, loud enough so I can hear it.

I pause outside the door, letting the rage simmer in my bones before I respond. Then I duck down so I can look him in the eyes. "You say that, but it didn't take you long to replace me."

He gives me a side look and shakes his head. "So fucking rich coming from you," he says.

I don't know what to say to that, so I don't say anything. I can't even slam the car door because it's a fucking gull wing.

It closes by itself, and he roars off back out the way he came.

Why did I say that? Where the hell are these infuriating emotions coming from?

The house is just waking up as I storm through the building. Staff are coming and going with breakfast trays. The dogs are going nuts as they get their morning feed. I make it to my room without seeing anyone else and slam the door. I lean against it, breathing, allowing my heart to get back to normal.

He's a distraction.

Forget about him.

After a few minutes, when my hands are no longer shaking, I retrieve my phone from its hiding place. I promptly check for messages, and I'm relieved to see there's a new addition to my document from Dante.

No sign of Rebecca.
 On my way back.

He's coming back, which is great timing since the party is later today. I could do with some support after the morning I've had. Adding Dante to the list of an already crazy selection of guests could be the end of me. But I need him. It scares me to acknowledge that.

Tonight is also the engagement announcement. I'm not stupid to think I have any control over who Adrien sells me to. There will be a closed bidding system of some kind, offering the family things he can't buy easily, like connections.

Unless Lorcan steps up to the plate, Kristian will probably win. I still haven't decided how I'm going to navigate this one. My father marrying me off isn't new. It's the reason I ran away in the first place. The weight of the anklet reminds me that's not an option now. Unless I find some way of getting this off, I'm trapped.

Dante might have a way.

Or I could just kill my father and be done with this whole fucking thing.

Plenty of options.

I glance at my watch. Time to get dressed. I pull on some jeans and a t-shirt and head downstairs. I'm hungry so I head to the kitchen. If I really wanted, I could place an order with one of the staff, but I'm not in the mood to talk to anyone. The kitchen is empty so I make myself some toast. I can't make much else. There are no knives or cooking utensils. All the catering comes from outside the estate and is delivered fresh every day. They bring their cutlery with them and take it away again. A ridiculous process to keep me from killing someone, given that Dante has smuggled me in so many weapons, knives included.

As I'm eating my toast, Dino walks in rubbing his neck. He looks like he hardly slept, although he was dead to the world when I left him at 6 a.m. this morning.

"I woke up and you weren't there," he says, furrowing his brow at me. He makes himself a piece of toast. Lorcan strolls in a few minutes later, keys in one hand, a tray of coffees in the other. He takes his sunglasses off and places the coffees on the table.

"Oat skinny latte and a macchiato," he says. Then picks one of the cups up and fucks off.

Just like old times.

Dino takes his macchiato and hands me the last cup which must be the oat latte. I take a sip. No sugar but a hint of caramel, just the way I like it.

"He'll come round once you tell him what you're really doing here," Dino says. "He thinks you don't care."

"He's right. I don't care." I finish my coffee and drop the paper cup into the trash before leaving the room. As fun as it is talking about Lorcan's emotions, I have things to do before tonight—namely finding where my father has taken Rebecca.

THIRTEEN

VIOLA

ADRIEN APPEARS to have organized a party not unlike the ones I was forced to attend as a twelve-year-old. Plenty of old men and young girls in sex kitten outfits. Only this time I have more than just my teeth and nails to keep me safe.

I'm wearing a clingy, black, all in one halterneck jump-suit with my hair tied back. It's my effort to be difficult to get into, and show-off/conceal as much as possible.

The dagger Dante gave me isn't in its usual place. I've hidden it in my ponytail so when Gigi pats me down with her bandaged hands as we enter the main room where the party is held, she finds absolutely fuck all.

"What a job to give someone with injured hands,' I say nonchalantly as she straightens up.

She glares at me. I cock my head waiting and eventually she steps aside so I can enter with Dino. I steer him to one side of the room which has a view of everyone, and an easy escape route.

"At least Kristian won't try anything on in here," Dino says, clocking powerful, rich, and famous men and women, those we see in our newspapers and on our TVs, sipping martinis and chatting shit amongst themselves.

So so so innocent Dino. Does he really think Kristian won't do what he wants with them watching? No-one here gives a fuck. They're all here to indulge in the worst of sins, hidden from public scrutiny. If Kristian wants to try and rape me, everyone here will watch thinking it's entertainment. Some might even join in.

I sigh and scan the room. I haven't seen my father yet.

Kristian is here and so is Griffin. Although Griffin looks nervous. I haven't seen him all day so I can only imagine he went home when some of the others did, not taking my father up on the offer to stay the night.

"I need to speak to him," I say to Dino. It was Griffin's men in the video. Surely, he would know where they took Rebecca.

"Want me to go and distract my brother?"

I shake my head. "Not yet." I'm drawn to where a group of men have gathered around a young girl. Long blonde hair, cherub face, glossy pink lips. She's wearing a short skirt, crop top, and pink converse with stars on. She looks about twelve herself. Although by my calculation she's seven years younger than me, so that makes her fifteen or sixteen. Thankfully not twelve.

She spots me and smiles broadly. Then she skips over.

Yes, skips.

"Who the hell is she?" Dino asks a second before she gets to us. I don't get to answer.

"Cousin V!" she shrieks. She throws her arms around me and hugs me. I'm stiff in her arms because she's the last person I was expecting to see tonight.

Lily Hawkes.

She gives Dino a once over, eyes popping out of her head. "Well, hello, gorgeous," Lily says. Dino just looks at her, a frown creasing his forehead. He shoots me a look that I can't decipher. *Does he want an introduction?*

"This is Lily. My cousin on my mother's side," I say blandly.

"Lovely to meet you Dino," she purrs, taking his hand in hers.

Dino's frown deepens and he opens his mouth, but no words come out.

"Why are you here?" I say to Lily.

"Uncle Adrien invited me. He sent a car round to the Old Vic." She looks around. "I was hoping to see Dante, is he here too?"

Lily has an obsession with Dante. I've no idea why.

"You need to leave," I say. I've no idea why Adrien invited her unless to make things more complicated. Kato should have made sure she was protected. Unless something has happened to Kato…

Fucking Kato. He promised he'd look after Rebecca's family.

Her brow creases slightly. "I don't think so. I only just got here. And Adrien said I could stay with you," she says. A waiter passes with a tray of drinks. She takes a glass of champagne off it and knocks it back. She side-eyes Dino with a grin and then grabs his crotch making him immediately splutter out his drink. "Or I could stay with you."

Kristian chooses that moment to look over, a creepy smile easing onto his face.

Oh no you don't.

"My room now," I say, hauling Lily away from Dino.

"Ow, what the fuck, V, you're hurting me." I ignore her and drag her down the corridor and into my room. Dino enters quickly behind us. "Shut the door," I say to him. I dump Lily on the bed and then root though my closet until I find something a little more suitable for a barely legal girl at a sex party.

"Here, put this on."

It's a pair of jeans and a hoodie.

Lily raises a brow and then starts to strip, making Dino turn the brightest shade of fucking red I've ever see.

"Dino, turn around for fuck's sake."

His eyes dart to me and then he abruptly turns to face the door. I don't need this stress right now, but I've no idea what to do. Lily is my mother's niece. I'm shit with kids, if I'm honest. Although Lily isn't a kid anymore. If Adrien brought her here from the Old Vicarage campus where she's supposed to be studying for her end of year exams, he must have done it to get at me.

"Do not leave this room," I say to her as I drag Dino outside with me. "How did you get here? Did you drive?" I ask him once we're outside the room and he's able to form words coherently.

"Finn drove," he says. "W—why?"

"I need you to go and find him, take Lily home," I say to him.

He shakes his head. "No way. She's fucking jailbait. I'm not getting into a car with her. She all but fucking molested me. Order her a taxi."

"She's legal," I say. *Barely*.

"Like fuck she is."

"She's just turned sixteen," I say, hoping that's true. "And if I get her a taxi, she'll ditch it and come back. Or worse, go elsewhere."

He scowls, dimple popping out. "Fine. I'll do it. But stay the fuck away from my brother. He's been eyeing you since we came down tonight." He takes out his phone and makes a call.

I take a breath and head back into the room, then I close it and stand in front of it. Lily is sitting on the end of the bed, watching me. She's put the hoodie on, but the jeans she slashed into hot pants. They were my favorite fucking ones. I glance down. She's still wearing her pink converse.

I sigh and she smirks, showing her age in her eyes. She plays her innocent card up more than I do. But Lily is far from innocent.

"He's gone, so tell me the truth. Why are you here, Lily?" I can't worry about my clothes now. Something doesn't add up. Lily is a spoilt brat, but she knows what these places are. She's not dumb. She wouldn't come here unless there was something in it for her.

"Adrien gave me a job," she says coyly, playing the hoodie tie string, wrapping it around her fingers.

"What kind of job?" I ask.

"Seduce Lorcan Duke," she says, head tilted.

"Lorcan wouldn't…" I tail off. *He wouldn't what Viola? Fuck a teenager? He's a teenager himself.*

"Wouldn't go for me? Are you sure? I look just his type," she says, innocently.

And she does, but also eight years too fucking young. "Trust me. You're nowhere near his type." *I'm his type, you little bitch.* I shake my head to clear my thoughts. *And soothe my nerves.* "Is that all?"

She gives a sigh. "Then I play victim. Adrien wants him gone. Say, arrested for sex with a minor?"

Fifteen then. Fucking hell. The lengths Adrien will go to.

"And Rebecca, where did Adrien get you to take her?" I knew it was Lily the moment I saw her on the security video. She had her hood up but I recognized her shoes.

"I don't remember," she smirks.

I clench my jaw. It's so hard to not do something I'll regret. I walk up to the little brat and take her by her throat. She grins, looking up at me with those big brown eyes. She has mine and my mother's eyes.

"I know it was you who went to Beckbridge house pretending to be me."

"Adrien knows I'm useful, unlike you." She looks me up and down as far as her gaze will go, given the position I've got her in. "Who's good for one thing only."

"What do you mean by that?"

She laughs so I squeeze until she chokes. I would love nothing more than to press down until she turns bloody blue.

"Lily, where did you take Rebecca?"

"I don't fucking know," she says. "All I did was wheel her into the van."

Then I do need to speak to Griffin.

I release my grip but before I let her go, I slip my free hand into her pocket and pull out a vial of clear liquid. When she was undressing, I saw her palm it and then slip it into her pocket.

"And this?"

Her gaze flicks to my hand and I loosen my grip so she can speak. "Just a little Love Tap for the Duke," she says grinning back at me.

"A date rape drug?" I shake my head. "Lily, who gave this to you?"

She zips up her mouth and throws away the key, all smiles without her teeth showing.

There's a knock on the door. *Finally, someone that fucking knocks.*

I let her go, dropping her onto the bed. "Dino is going to take you home." Lorcan isn't getting within three feet of this girl.

Her face brightens up. "Is he the fuckable redhead?"

I ignore her question, take the vial and put it into my own pocket.

There are red marks on her neck where I held her. I know I should feel bad about that but I don't. She makes no move to ease them. She's been through worse. We all have.

There's another knock.

"Come in," I say, turning around.

Finn, Dino, and Lorcan walk in. I give Dino a look to say, 'Why the fuck is Lorcan here?' but he doesn't seem to notice. Dino's eyes dart between me and Lily who is still half sprawled on the bed. "I brought everyone."

Lorcan gives me a cool, callous look, and then darts a gaze to Lily. "Your cousin?"

I sigh and nod, turning to Dino and Finn. "Can I trust you two to get her home," I say, looking at them both.

"I'd rather stay here," Lily says, staring at them all almost star struck. "With him." She smiles at Lorcan.

"Well, you can't. You're going home with the fuckable redhead instead," I say.

She shrugs. "Fine by me."

Lorcan frowns, Finn snorts a laugh, and Dino just looks confused.

"Come on," Dino says, letting out a breath. He walks over and guides Lily out by her shoulders. As he passes me, he pauses.

"Lorcan's going to stay with you in case Kristian comes back while I'm gone."

"Just don't let Lily out of your sight," I reply.

After they've gone, It's just me and Lorcan.

Alone.

"For someone who wants nothing to do with me, you're doing a pretty piss poor job of it."

Lorcan narrows his eyes and glares, then after a few seconds exhales. "Dino told me why you stayed. Why didn't you tell me?"

"I didn't tell Dino so that he could bring you into it," I say. *Didn't you? They tell each other everything.*

"You should have told me," he says, shoving his hands in his pockets.

I don't know what to say to that, so I just stare at him. I never agreed to tell him everything. All three of them barged into my life and the rules never got discussed. And I need rules. Dante understands that. This messy, emotional shit makes no fucking sense. Especially when I don't even know if I'm starting to feel things, or if I'm just evolving into an even more fucked-up monster.

"I don't have to tell you everything," I say, shutting down.

Lorcan shakes his head and gives a harsh laugh, flicking his eyes heavenward. "You never give in do you?"

"It's the way I am." *Accept it or fuck off.*

He pauses and then nods. "I guess I can deal with that. But what I'm not good with is seeing you hurt those I care about."

"I didn't know asking Dino to get close to his brother would break him. I'm not good with understanding emotions." Dino doesn't even look broken. He's still the same. He's still annoying and protective as hell.

He snorts. "At least we agree on something."

There's another shitty silence.

"Is this the moment where you walk away?" I ask.

He stares back, brow furrowed but the rest of his face unreadable, and then he sighs. "Look, I came because I want to help find

Rebecca. I miss you like fucking crazy and I'm jealous as hell, but I'll put all that aside to help you. Just like you helped me."

"Okay," I say, for want of something better. "You don't have to stay with me. Kristian won't try anything. He won't want to piss off my father."

"Just be fucking careful around Sinner, because you're not the one who's going to have to pick up the pieces after you're gone."

I take him in, the boy I stalked all those months ago. He seems older, and wiser. It's turning me the fuck on. If I'm honest, there's a gaping hole inside me, a void that won't go away ever since I left the boys and moved back home.

I've been trying to ignore it for fucking months.

And now, I'm tired.

I nod. "Okay, but I'm taking Kristian and my father out," I say. "And I need Griffin on board with it. He knows where Rebecca is."

Lorcan raises a brow. "Sounds like we're aligned for once. Leave Graham Baron to me."

"You think you can convince him to tell you?"

"He's Finn's uncle."

I've no idea what that means, but I'm glad of the alliance.

"You need anything else?"

"Do you have access to Joseph's money?"

He indicates that he does with a nod.

"Then I need that money you once offered me." I need enough to take Rebecca far away from here. And I need a new identity. One that's completely untraceable and will pass every goddamn test there is.

Unfortunately, those don't come cheap.

FOURTEEN

VIOLA

AFTER LORCAN LEAVES, I take my phone out of its hiding place and check for any messages in the vault. I'm about to call Dante when the door bursts open. Dino and Finn are back already, minus Lily. They haven't even been gone ten minutes.

"Viola, your cousin gave us the slip," Dino says, coming in, running his hand through his hair as he looks around the room.

"She didn't by any chance come back here, did she?" asks Finn, coming in and closing the door behind him.

I place a hand on my hip. "Why would she come back here?" They both look at me blankly. I feel my pocket for the vial of drugs. It's gone.

"For fuck's sake. She's underage and she's walking around armed with liquid E."

Dino glares at me. "Fucking hell, Viola. You said she was sixteen."

"Why does she have E?" Finn asks.

"She's planning to date rape Lorcan," I say, ignoring Dino's remark.

"You Hawkes girls are fucking crazy bitches." Finn chuckles.

"Just find her so I don't have to fucking worry about her." I chase them out and then walk back into my room to call Dante. It goes through to voicemail so I leave a message.

"Where the fuck are you? Lily's here and Griffin knows where Rebecca is," I hiss into the recorder.

"I'm right here," says a deep voice. I spin around, seeing him close the door behind him and lean against it, casually holding some chicken wire and electrical tape.

Kristian.

"Well that was fun." He smirks. "You don't look like you scare easily."

"You just startled me." I indicate to the items in his hands. "Been raiding the garden shed have you?"

He takes the chicken wire and starts looping it over the door handle to lock it. He's humming while he does it, flashing me dashing smiles every once in a while, as he looks up. Then he starts walking toward me, still fucking humming.

"Adrien warned you not to do this." I take a step back, slipping my phone into my pocket.

"He did. But the deal is pretty much done. You're as good as mine," he says softly.

I could fight him, but I'm not dumb enough to think he won't overpower me easily. *The window is behind me. That would be a better choice. It's not too much of a drop to the ground floor and once I'm out I can make a run for it.*

He lunges just as I reach the window and drags me back. I throw my head back, breaking his nose but he picks me up and throws me onto the bed.

I don't waste time catching my breath, I reach for the blade in my ponytail and slash it at him as soon as he comes near me, cutting some of my hair off in the process. I feel it kiss flesh as I shove myself as far as I can go, against the headboard.

"You fucking bitch," Kristian snarls. There's blood down one side of his cheek, messing his pretty face up. "I'm so going to enjoy fucking you up."

"That should be my line," I say, finally allowing the red rage in to cloud my vision. I've been keeping it at bay for so long, I've forgotten how good it feels.

Kristian reaches for my legs and yanks me toward him, grabbing my hand as he does. He twists my wrist hard, and the crack of bone comes before the stabbing pain. I drop the knife and he pins me to the bed by sitting on my fucking chest, unmovable no matter how hard I try to buck him off. As he hauls my arms above my head, holding me down, I start to scream.

I'm not above screaming.

It's useful.

Like now.

The door to my room kicks open and several of Adrien's men barge in, all with guns aimed at Kristian's head. As they demand he lets me go, he starts laughing. He leans close and bites my ear hard enough to leave teeth marks. "On our wedding night, I'm going to rape you and make Dino watch," he says.

"That'll be hard to do if Adrien kills you."

"Mr. Vice, we won't ask you again to remove yourself from Miss Hawkes."

He chuckles like it's the most hilarious thing, and then lifts himself off me. Adrien's men escort him out.

I sit up, clutching my fucking broken wrist like a wounded bird. Dante is standing in the doorway, arms crossed, a look of utter dismay on his face.

"You finally turned up?'

"Have I taught you nothing?"

"The bed is too fucking soft for a sweep," I snap at him.

"Stay here, I'll get one of Adrien's medics."

"No, I'll go myself. Just help me up."

He sighs, comes into the room and offers a hand. I take it with my good arm and he lifts me up with ease. At that moment, Lorcan and Dino turn up. The look on their faces when they see Dante helping me off the bed is priceless.

"What the fuck?" Dino pants, out of breath like he's been running. "Viola, are you okay?"

"I'm fine," I say.

"We heard screaming." Lorcan gives Dante a hostile look. "What did you fucking do to her?"

I roll my eyes. "Nothing. He's just helping me up."

Dante stares at the boys and then shakes his head at me. "You said you were done with this, V."

"You're the one she should be fucking done with," Lorcan says gruffly.

Dante's mouth curls up into an evil smile. "Is that so?"

"Oh, for fuck's sake," I say. I close my eyes and then open them again. Nope. They're all still here, pissing over each other like a bunch of fucking tom cats. "I'm going to get my wrist looked at. Stay here."

None of them listen to me. All three follow me down to the treatment room Adrien uses for his physio. I draw the line at them all coming in with me, crowding it. I make them wait outside. It doesn't take long for the medic to bound my wrist in a splint. It's a clean break.

When I come out, Lorcan and Dante are nowhere to be seen, only Dino is left waiting with a bottle of water.

"All good?" he asks, stepping forward.

"Doctor said I should get it x-rayed but fuck that," I say, trying to open a packet of pain killers. I'm going to need something stronger when it wears off. Dino ends up opening the packet for me.

I take a few pills with some water, clearing my throat. "Did you find Lily yet?" I ask. If he has, that's one less problem I have to worry about.

"Finn is still looking for her," Dino says.

"And Griffin? Did Lorcan get Rebecca's location off him?"

Dino nods. "Dante and Lorcan are going there now."

I raise both brows. "Together?" Did I step into an alternate universe or something?

"It wasn't mutual. Neither of them trusts the other one."

Okay. That makes more sense. Suddenly the room spins and I feel extremely tired. I stumble into Dino. He zooms in and out of focus as he grabs hold of me.

"Did you fucking drug me again, Sinner?" I slur.

"No, of course not."

I blink at him, noticing the bottle of water he's holding. It's water from the fridge in my father's office. "Who gave you that?"

"I did," says Gigi as she walks with a beautiful limp down the corridor with a smug smile plastered on her face. The men who saved me from Kristian are with her too. Only now, they have their guns pointed at Dino and me. "Your father wants you in his office now."

"She's going fucking nowhere with you," Dino says, stepping in front to protect me, but it's the wrong move. Several men also step forward, guns raised.

"Really? You'd die for her?" Gigi asks him, an incredulous look on her face.

"In a heartbeat," Dino snarls.

She doesn't like that answer. Clearly, no one has ever stepped in front of a gun for her. But Dino doesn't see the guy behind him moving in, and I'm much too slow with whatever it is in my system to warn him.

It all sort of happens in slow motion.

The guy whacks him over the head. Dino goes down like a sack of bricks. And two of Adrien's men seize my arms to keep me from falling flat on my face.

"I'm going to finish what Dante started," I say. "And burn the rest of you."

"Poor Viola," Gigi says, grabbing my chin to make me look up at her. "Did you really think Griffin would betray your father like that? Dante can't help you now. Pretty soon, he'll be dead. Just like all the rest."

I spit in her face, and she grins.

"Bring her," Gigi barks and I can do nothing but let them drag me down the corridor toward my father. Strangely, I'm not thinking about killing Adrien or finding Rebecca. Or even burning Gigi alive. I'm worrying about Dino on the floor, and the trap Dante and Lorcan are walking into.

The last thing on my mind as the main room looms and I see my father standing next to a deranged looking Kristian as he holds Lily hostage…is that I never got to tell Dante the truth.

FIFTEEN

DANTE

THE LAST PLACE I want to be is in a sports car with some prick who can't drive behind the wheel, but Lorcan refused to get into my Mustang, so here we are.

He keeps glancing at me, wary, like I might attack him at any moment.

It's almost comical.

"Do you love her," he eventually says. I stare at him for a few minutes trying to understand what the hell he's saying. "I'm not speaking Irish, mate. I asked you a fucking question."

I don't understand what she sees in him, but I'll humor her while she goes through this phase.

If I fucking must.

"Love is an illusion," I say finally.

Lorcan snorts. "Fucking idiot. You have no idea what you have with her, do you?"

I clench my jaw and then force myself to relax it, cracking my neck to get the ache out. "And you do? Didn't you drop her the moment things got difficult?"

Lorcan's gaze hardens, and his hands tighten on the steering wheel, but he doesn't say anything else. That seems to have shut the little prick up.

The address Griffin gave Lorcan is on the other side of the county, but I see it as soon as we get a few miles in—a reflection of the streetlights on the paintwork dipping in and out indicating someone is tailing us.

I glance in the rearview mirror again, just to be sure. "We're being followed," I say to Lorcan.

He frowns and looks to where my gaze is locked. After a few seconds, he sees it too. "Son of a bitch."

"I know this area," I say. "There's a turning into a farm up ahead, once you get around the corner take it and turn everything off."

Lorcan does as I tell him, and we wait in darkness and silence for the car with no headlights to move past.

"Why the fuck would…"

"V's in trouble," I say.

"We should go back," he says. I don't argue with him. "I'll kill Adrien myself," he mutters as he starts the car.

V can also handle herself. I know. I trained her. Although lately, she's gotten sloppy. She's making mistakes like she's seeking them out. I brought her back to end this, but she's hesitating. Rebecca is an excuse. She knows that and so do I. I've let this go on much too long.

Adrien needs to go.

I was hoping V would have gotten her shit together by now and dealt with him.

I pick up my phone as Lorcan drives back the way we came. There are a lot of unread messages. Just seeing them makes my skin crawl and my fingers itch to read them, but the moment I do, my clients expect me to respond. If I'm unavailable, I'm working —on a job. That's the rule I keep with them. And it works when I'm on top of things.

Goddammit.

Her disorder is creeping into my domain. I need to end this so that I can move forward. I ignore them all and find her number and call it.

After a minute it goes through to voicemail.

Lorcan glances at me. "She picking up?"

"No," I say. But that doesn't mean anything.

"So, what's the plan?"

I stare straight ahead, feeling the pressure building inside my chest. The familiar pull whenever V is involved. I look over at Lorcan who seems to be waiting for me to take the lead.

"Pull over," I say when I see my car on the side of the road. I get out, pop open the trunk and take out the case filled with guns. Then I get back in his car.

"The plan is"—I open the case to check I have everything I need, then I close it, shooting a look at Lorcan—"we kill them all."

SIXTEEN

VIOLA

WHEN I WAKE UP, I'm stiff and my head is throbbing. So is my wrist. I'm also dying of thirst.

The first thing clear from the sounds and smells, is that I'm not at my father's estate. I'm in a bedroom with hideous mirrored furniture and monochrome walls. I'm wearing nothing but my underwear and the splint on my wrist. The tracker is still around my ankle, but the light is green.

I have no idea where the fuck I am. But I know I'm not at home. My father sold me to Kristian. That's all I remember. This must be the Vice residence in Chelsea. Adrien must have given Kristian the device that controls the tracker so he could move me from the estate.

There's a sound of classical music and…soft sobbing coming through the walls. I get out of bed, holding my wrist because its fucking killing me now, and walk over to door. It's locked. Of course it would be. I peer through the keyhole and try to see outside the room I'm in but all I can see is the floral wallpaper of the hallway and not much else.

I want to try kicking the door down but if I do, I'll alert Kris-

tian to the fact that I'm awake, and I want to assess my situation before I have to fight him a little more.

I don't believe for a second Dante and Lorcan are dead. They may have walked into a trap, but I know Dante—he's been in worse situations.

Dino is fine because he's Kristian's brother.

And Jude, I hope is still safe and sound in juvie.

Since when did I start collecting people to care about?

I glance about the room looking for something to use as a weapon. There isn't anything but a bed, bedsheets, a chest of drawers, and a bathroom off to the side. There's nothing in the drawers and the bathroom has the minimum—toilet paper and sanitary towels. Nothing else.

Voices in the hallway bring me back into the main room. There's shouting and banging, Then a door slams and someone walks away. The sobbing continues, getting louder. There's someone in the next room. I put my ear to the wall between my room and theirs and listen.

It might be Lily. But I never pegged her for the crying type.

"Shut the fuck up. Stop whining, you're driving me crazy," a female voice hisses.

Okay, that's Lily. I give a knock. "Lily, is that you?" I say in a low voice.

The crying suddenly stops. "Cousin V!"

It's Lily alright. The fucker brought her here? Why? The deal was for me alone. The buzzing under my skin is back. I don't know if I'm angry about Lily being here, or just that I'm stuck here as helpless as my mother was. All the same, I feel the urge to do some violence.

Some absolute fucking carnage.

"Are you hurt?" I force myself to speak, breathing in and out.

"No, we're not hurt."

We. She's not alone. "We? Who is there with you?"

"There's two of us. Some girl I don't know who won't stop fucking crying."

"Pascal," says a second voice with a higher pitch.

"Your name's Pascal?" I hear Lily say.

The girl must nod, because I don't hear anything after that.

"Is there anything in there you can use as a weapon?" I say through the wall to them.

"I already looked. Nothing," Lily answers.

What does Kristian want with an underage teenage girl?

The sobbing starts up again as footsteps resound in the hall. Someone is coming. The girl in the room with Lily begins to whimper. I hear Lily tell her to stop being a little bitch just as the door to my room unlocks and swings open. I'm still on the floor next to the wall so I back up into a crouch. Kristian strolls in, an evil looking smile on his face.

Red hair, sparkling blue eyes—he looks so much like Dino, it's sickening.

"How's my little bitch this morning?"

I get to my feet. I will myself not to react. Fighting him now, with a broken wrist, when I don't know the layout of the house or where the device is that controls my tracker, is futile. Still, the rage inside me unfurls like an animal. All claws and fucking fire. I snarl at him, letting him see the beast.

He smirks and comes over, grabbing my hair, yanking it back and forcing me to look into his eyes. He looks me up and down, assessing my body. There's no heat in his gaze. It's like he's assessing a horse for purchase.

"Adrien won't give you his empire," I say. "He's using you to break me."

"Oh, but he already has," he says. "We signed last night." He pulls my head to the side until the breath of his mouth is hot on my ear. "As long as I breed you and give him a grandson, he'll give me the whole goddamn thing."

Red hot rage screams through me. With my free hand I grab and twist part of him that would render any man in extreme pain. Kristian sucks the air between his teeth, eyes rolling back in his head, and then he groans.

"Fuck, baby. That's what I've been waiting for." When I glare at him, he chuckles. "Did my brother not tell you how much I like pain? We both do. That's why we have so many scars."

The sobbing next door suddenly starts up again, louder this time. And then I hear Lily scream.

I stiffen at the noise.

"My boys won't hurt them if you do what the fuck I say. You're here to be my broodmare, nothing else."

He lets go of my hair and seizes me by my broken wrist. I don't cry out, but my eyes water. The pain is excruciating as he shoves me into the wall and presses my head against it.

I can hear Lily screaming on the other side of it.

"Listen," he says. "Listen fucking hard. Because if I want you to sit on my lap, you'll do it. If I want you to suck me off while I enjoy a glass of Chianti, you will. If I want to fuck you in front of my goddamn friends, you'll bloody well let me."

"I will eviscerate you," I snarl.

He licks the side of my cheek, then he grabs my face and twists my head toward him. "Fight me if you can, love. I do love a good fight."

He has my broken wrist in one hand and my head pressed against the wall with the other. He's bigger in every fucking way. But I'm not like the women he's used to. I use every muscle in my body to smash my forehead into his already broken nose. He grunts and throws me against the bed frame. I slam against it, the impact forcing the air from my lungs. Pain slices through my arm as I land on it awkwardly, but then I'm scrabbling to turn around.

He's on top of me before I can blink. He hauls me onto the bed by my hair and then shoves my face into the pillow. I kick and bite but it's no use. I can't fucking breathe. Rage burns every part of me awake as I struggle to find an opening. He can't kill me. He needs me. As my lungs scream for air and adrenaline sends my body into panic mode, I float away until I'm no longer part of what's happening.

There's pressure on my back and a hand locks around my

good arm, bending it behind me. It frees my head so I can lift it slightly. I turn it sideways and drag in a breath.

He crouches over until his lips are so close that they graze my ear as he speaks. "Threatening young girls doesn't seem to be enough for you. Maybe I'll kill one of your pretty boys? Which one shall I pick? I know, how about Jude? I've always hated that little cocksucker."

"You fucking dare," I hiss, struggling to get free so I can rip him apart.

"I can and I will. I give the word and Griffin will order his execution. Griffin will do anything to get back his sweet, tender Pascal."

"Jude can take care of himself," I say.

"What about my brother? There are things I could do to him that will make him wish he'd never been born. And the best part? He'll only blame himself."

I stop moving. I stop trying to fight.

The darkness wants to take over.

I claw it back, inch by inch.

I can't lose them all.

I just can't.

"Good girl," he says and pats me on the cheek.

Kristian releases me and gets off the bed. I take a few breaths before turning onto my back. My vision is filled with dark spots as I blink against the light. My wrist is in fucking agony but all I do is hold it against my chest and give Kristian a dark look.

"I'm going to kill you in the worst possible way," I say.

"You're fucking hilarious," he says, eyes twinkling with delight. His nose is bleeding, and his blue suit is rumpled. He makes no move to straighten up. All he does is run his fingers through his messy hair, smoothing it over. He looks down where I am on the bed. "Too bad I had to fuck up your wrist again. That'll heal badly."

Then he's gone.

So that's why the other girl is in the room with Lily. Why is Kristian collecting leverage from everyone? Is that my father's doing?

I crawl toward the end of the bed with one hand clutched to my chest. Then I slip my feet under me to rest them on the floor.

"Lily," I say in a low voice. When she doesn't answer, I shuffle closer and rest my head on the wall, enjoying the way the painted plaster feels cool on my forehead.

"Lily," I say again. "Are you hurt?" I need her not to be hurt so I can get her out of here alive. But there's nothing but silence from the girls next door.

SEVENTEEN

VIOLA

"PASCAL," I say, trying Griffin's niece.

"Lily isn't waking up," a terrified voice says through the wall. I clench my jaw against another wave of pain and suck in a breath of air.

"Is she breathing," I say tersely. I remember seeing a couple of over-the-counter painkillers in the bathroom.

"Yes, she's breathing."

"Okay, good. Put her in the recovery position while I go into the bathroom."

"Wait, don't leave us."

"I'm not leaving," I grit out, closing my eyes and then opening them again as the pain erodes away my patience. One thing is true—I absolutely hate kids.

After I find the painkillers, I settle onto the floor next to the wall facing the door and listen for Lily waking up. Every so often Pascal asks me if I'm there and I say, "Yes, I am." And then we lapse into silence again.

It gets dark fast. Eventually, Lily wakes up and wants a burger.

I check she's okay, as much as I can by asking.

She's subdued, but she says she's fine. If she says so then she must be. I can't read between the lines at the best of times, and clocking her body language is out of the question.

"Do you still have the liquid E?" I ask her just after the man outside leaves and before the next one arrives. In my head I've worked out the rota of the guards on the doors and how many. One usually, two at most. They're cocky bastards who think with their dicks more than anything.

"Er, yes, it's up my vag? Why?" Lily says.

"Just hold on to it."

"Fine. I was hoping to trade it for a burger," Lily snorts.

I roll my eyes. She has the appetite of a horse. I don't blame her though. So far, they've fed us twice. Once at what felt like midday, and then later just after sunset. They do it in pairs and I have to sit on the bed while they slide the tray through the door and into the room. They don't give me anything that could be used as a weapon. Just a tray of sandwiches, a box of juice with a paper straw, and some more pain killers. I'm used to a light diet, but Lily hasn't stopped complaining. She reminds me of Jude.

Fuck, I miss him.

Long after the girls have fallen asleep, when my wrist has settled to a dull ache thanks to the drugs, and there's no sign of Kristian, I let myself drift. The dreams I have are dark and full of fucking blood. More often than not, I wake to Lily asking me if I'm okay.

I forgot that I do that—shout in my sleep.

Only the boys know about that little quirk of mine, and they never say a fucking word.

The next day is much the same. Guards changing, bland food arriving, and no Kristian. On the outside I appear sane and calm, but inside I'm seething. It's like a black hole has opened up inside me and everything I am is being consumed into it. I'm becoming this dark, soulless thing with only one desire—to slice Kristian into little pieces and feed him to my father's fucking dogs.

After two more days, the girls are getting restless. So am I. I don't see the need to sit by the wall anymore, so I use the time and the facilities wisely. There's a shower so I use it. My demand for clean clothes goes ignored. The underwear I'm wearing still has spots of Kristian's blood on it, but I'd rather wear it than be naked.

I've stopped taking the painkillers. My wrist is less painful day by day though it's still quite sore. Lily occasionally cracks a joke through the wall but mostly I leave them to chat amongst themselves. I spend every moment looking for weaknesses, especially in the windows (which have bars) and the door. I stress the furniture in case it could be broken easily. I save up my painkillers just in case. And I pace the fucking room looking for any way out.

Occasionally, I cut myself with my nails and leave drops of blood under the mat and behind mirrors. Should anyone come looking for me, it's useful for them to know I was here. If I die, at least the police might find my blood all over this room.

On the fourth day of being in this shitty room, I've had enough. I stalk up the door and bang on it.

"Bill, I need more meds," I say through the door to the guy outside. I've chosen to target Bill because he's the quieter one. He's also the one who speaks to us with a kinder voice. I know his name because I've heard the others call him it occasionally. Bill doesn't answer at first. He probably doesn't know what to do or say now that I'm talking to him.

"Bill? Are you there?" I say again, giving a gentle tap. "I'm in a lot of pain." It's not a lie. Since I've stopped taking the drugs they give me with every meal, I've been in downright agony.

Both Lily and Pascal have stopped talking. I wish they would bloody act normal because they're making this a bigger deal than it is.

"I can't get you any more," he says, eventually.

"Can I at least have another glass of water?" I ask. "Please, I'm parched." I've been drinking out of the bathroom tap, but hopefully Bill doesn't know that.

After a few seconds, Lily pipes up. "Can I get one too Bill? My mouth is like the Sahara."

For fuck's sake, Lily. I'm ready to try another tactic when there's the sound of Bill shifting in his chair, getting to his feet.

"Alright, but just one glass each," he says gruffly.

I peer through the keyhole to see him pass in front of my door, then I hear him disappearing down the hall.

As soon as he's gone, I waste no time. I walk into the bathroom and start filling the toilet with tissue paper until the whole thing is plugged solid, then I open the cistern and wedge the flush down. It doesn't take long for water to come cascading over the top of the bowl and start flooding the bathroom.

By the time Bill comes back, water is pouring into the main room. I stay in the bathroom when he tells me to get on the bed and unlocks the door to come in.

I can see him through the crack between the door hinges looking confused. "Bill, a pipe has burst in the bathroom!" I shout.

He puts the glass on the side and hurries into the bathroom to take a look. I step out from behind the door and I hit him over the head with the cistern lid, knocking him out cold. The pain wrenching through my injured arm has me gasping, but I can't sit and cry. I have to keep moving.

Keys first.

I fumble for them with one hand in his pocket. The other I shove under my arm pit to take the edge off how much it fucking kills.

"You bastard," I say when the keys slip into the water pooling around my feet and his prone body on the bathroom floor. I stick my hand in and fish about, finally grasping them.

"V, what's happening?" Lily says through the wall.

I don't have time to explain. I move quietly out into the hallway, checking to see that no one else is coming. Then I open the door to their room. Lily's eyes widen when she sees me. She jumps to her feet and so does the girl next to her. Apart from the cut on Lily's head, they look fine. And they're in actual fucking clothes.

"Why are you butt naked?" she asks as I usher her out into the hallway.

I shoot my eyes heavenward. "Just give me your hoodie." I know she has a t-shirt on underneath, because they're my clothes that I gave her. Lily is in the same clothes as she was the day of the party. She hauls it off and helps me put it over my head. Then I quietly make my way downstairs with the girls following.

There's no one in the main atrium when we get to the base of the stairs. Without a weapon I feel naked, never mind look it. *Fuck it.* I stalk up to the front door and try it but it's locked.

"Fuck," I say.

"Try Bill's keys," Lily says.

One of them works, and as soon as the door opens, I glance back at Lily.

"Once you get to the main road, stay out of sight. Don't flag any of the cars. Keep to the side roads until you get across the bridge, then find a pay phone or flag a black cab," I say. "Don't go back to school. Find Dante."

"You're not coming with us?" she asks.

"Do I look like I can come with you?" I say, indicating to the tracker on my ankle. It's beeping red.

She scowls but doesn't have time to say anything else because I'm shoving her out the door and locking it back up again. Now to get a fucking weapon and paint this fucking house red with his blood.

EIGHTEEN

DINO

LILY TURNING up at the frat house is the last thing I'd expect.

"Where's Dante?" she asks stepping inside.

"He's in the kitchen."

She rolls her eyes at me and saunters into the main open plan kitchen dining area. As soon as he sees her, he frowns. "I told you to go back to school."

"V told me not to," she says. "Anyway, this is where the party is." She flicks a dirty gaze to Lorcan when she sees him. "I'm here to help you get V back."

"You can help by going back to school," I say.

To me, her lips curl into a dark smile. "Maybe if I had you to help me with my homework, I would."

"Lily, you can't stay here," says Dante. "When Kato gets here, you're leaving with him."

She glowers at him. "I told you where she was and now you're shutting me out of the best fucking part."

After Lily called Dante, she promptly told him where to find Viola. She wasn't at Kristian's apartment in Sloane Square or the family house in Chelsea. It was like she'd vanished into thin air.

Five fucking days we've been looking for her. Anything could have happened.

I glance down at my phone. There's a new message from Kristian.

> *Family dinner at 8p.m.*
> *Aunt Helen's place.*
> *Bring an expensive bottle.*

Fucking finally. He's been avoiding me since that night at Harper-Black estate. I've been stonewalled at every goddamn place he frequents. Not one of the guys would talk to me and tell me what the fuck is going on.

And now Lily has told us where to find Viola, he messages me this.

Aunt Helen's place is code for one of the safe houses. Our families have a few of them dotted around the city. I don't know them all, but I do know this one and it matches the description of where Lily said she came from when she escaped.

'Why are we waiting for Kato anyway?" Lorcan asks.

"Backup," says Dante.

"Fuck backup," says Lorcan.

"It's better we stick to the plan," Dante says. Dante has been stalking the streets at night. I've no idea where he goes but he's always here in the morning ready with a cup of coffee and a dark psychotic look on his face. Lorcan doesn't trust him and neither do I, but Lily and Viola do so here we are.

"I don't give a fuck; we've waited hours already."

"You don't just stroll up and knock on the door," says Dante.

"Or maybe you do?" I say. "Maybe we want to wait before we barge in there," I say, showing the room my phone.

Dante's brow raises. "Your brother has invited you for dinner?"

"Nah, fuck that. We're going now," Lorcan says. The poor bastard looks terrible. He hasn't shaved, showered, or changed since the night of Adrien's party. I don't even know if he's had any sleep. Not that any of us have.

"Fine," Dante says. "It's your funeral."

Lorcan snorts and storms out. "Fucking pussy." A minute later the front door slams.

"Give him five minutes," I say. "He'll calm down."

Dante shrugs.

"Do you think he's like that in bed?" Lily asks.

I stare at her until there's a knock at the door and I use that as my excuse to leave the room. Kato and his men are waiting outside. I let him in, and a discussion recommences on the best way to take Kristian out given Griffin has firmly chosen a side.

"You'd think he'd switch sides after what Kristian did to Pascal," Lily mutters.

"You'd think," I say, agreeing with her.

Ten minutes later Lorcan returns, a lot less angry than when he left, with a chilled bottle of wine wrapped in tissue paper. He hands it to me.

"There. It's all they had in the liquor store in the high street," he says.

I glance down. "Château Margaux. Not bad." I lean in. "Kristian is going to know I'm not there for dinner," I say.

"Who gives a fuck what he thinks," says Lorcan. "She belongs to us." After a pause he glances at Dante and adds. "All of us."

I look up and catch Dante's eye. He nods when he sees the bottle. Lily smirks and stalks up to me.

"Can I be your date?" she asks, linking her arm through mine.

I furrow my brow at her. "Fuck no."

The house seems like an ordinary townhouse in Marylebone. To look at it you wouldn't think Viola was inside being held hostage. Five fucking days. I dread to think what might have happened in that time. I'm standing alone at the door waiting to be let inside.

There's a camera in the corner of the doorway so I know Kristian is watching me, trying to make me sweat.

Dante, Lorcan, and the rest are farther down the street waiting for my signal—that Viola is inside. If she's not, I'm going to skin Kristian alive. Viola doesn't belong to him. Maybe she never belonged to us, but she sure damn well doesn't belong to my fucked-in-the-head brother.

Viola deserves more than that.

A lot more.

One of Kristian's heavies opens the door after ten whole minutes. He grunts at me to come inside, checking behind me to see that there's no one on the street. Then he pats me down, taking the gun I have under my suit jacket. Kato gave it to me as we drove here, but like Viola, I fucking hate guns. Kristian killed our father with one. They make death easy, and killing should never be taken lightly.

I follow him inside. The place is sparsely decorated. Monochrome. Not my taste at all. Definitely Kristian's. I enter the open plan dining room which is white walls, a black leather sofa and a stark white coffee table on one side, and a shiny white kitchen with black metal fittings on the other. In the middle dividing the room is a black rectangular dining table made of metal and glass, and six black leather chairs around it.

Viola is sitting in one of the chairs looking for the world like the most devastatingly beautiful girl on earth. She's wearing a gold and black corset dress that wraps around one shoulder with full skirts. Her hair is loose, and her lips are glossy and ripe for kissing. She looks a million dollars. She doesn't look like she's a hostage until I see the bandage on her wrist; is dirty and there's bruises around her neck. He's painted over the cracks. He's made her look pretty on the outside, but he's treated her like shit. Just like he does with every girl my brother finds. He takes independent, strong women, and breaks them down until they're nothing. Then he forgets he even owns them and moves on to his next victim.

Viola gives me a blank look, but it's not a broken or an empty one. She's still fighting. And I love that about her. Even though I know that Kristian kills the women who won't break. That's what happened to Nancy, his ex wife. And what's going to happen to Viola if I don't get her away from him soon.

"Baby brother, welcome to our home," says Kristian. I didn't even notice him sitting at the far end of the table until he stands up. I shift my gaze to Viola as he comes over to kiss me on the cheek Italian style. "Little Sword has brought us some fucking good wine," he exclaims as he takes the bottle from my hands and examines it.

Our mother's side of the family is from Italy. That's where I got my nickname Dino. I was my mother's 'little sword'. I was the one always trying to protect her from our father. Since my mother is a crazy bitch who still prefers me to him, my brother likes to remind me at every turn. He uses it now to distract me. I'm hot and irritated inside, but I can't show that to Kristian until I've let the others know Viola is here.

"You're calling a safe house your home now? Why did you bring *Viola* here?" I say, trying to keep my face neutral.

Kristian's smile stays firmly in place as he opens the wine and pours out three even glasses. "You know how I like to have a little solitude. And we've had that in spades, haven't we, baby?" he says, eyes brighter and shinier than they should be. He's usually on something.

He offers me a glass of wine and indicates to a seat opposite Viola. I take it, giving Viola an intense look, hoping she realizes I have a plan. I haven't just turned up to hope for the best. I've just said the code word, *her name*, out loud so that Lorcan can hear. Before I entered the house, I called Lor and kept the line open so that they can listen to everything. Dante, Lorcan, and even Kato should be breaking the door down any fucking minute.

I need to act normal until they do.

Viola stares back as I break contact and force myself to look at

Kris, who has taken a seat next to Viola and takes a sip of his own drink.

"You left me to clean up your fucking mess, you mean," I say, ignoring my sweaty palms, forcing myself to relax my clenched jaw.

Kristian frowns, running his eyes over me. "And what's the problem? Griffin's boys haven't stopped distribution." He places his wine down and leans back, eyes on me.

"Our business with Duke—"

"Is redundant. He runs the cathouses and the fucked-up boarding school circuits just like his daddy, and we take care of the hard stuff. I don't see what the problem is, little brother." He eyeballs me and then laughs, shaking his head. "Only that you're his fucking bum buddy and you think you can come in here and take what's rightfully mine."

Viola's hand reaches forward and tightens around the stem of the remaining glass of wine as it rests on the table. There's no cutlery on the table. Just plates, glasses, and some kind of finger food. Viola is right to see the glass as a weapon. It's the only thing in the room apart from the candlesticks in the middle of the table that she could grab in a hurry.

Kristian sees it too and yanks Viola back by her hair. His motion knocks over the glass in her hand. She manages to smash and grab hold of it until he casually sticks a knife to her throat. I'm already on my feet.

"Don't move," Kristian says, eyes on me. As red wine pools all over the table and onto the white carpeted floor, Viola also looks my way. She's not making a sound. She also doesn't move either. My nostrils flare and my heart slams in my fucking chest, but I hold up a hand to calm my brother down. Kristian won't hesitate to kill her. Viola...I've no idea what she's going to do. I could do with backup right about now. *Where the fuck are the others?* As if to answer my question, my phone in my pocket vibrates. Something is wrong. If someone is trying to call me something is very fucking wrong. *Shit. The line was either disconnected or there's a bigger problem.*

But now I know for certain.

They're not coming.

"I haven't shoved my dick inside this one yet. I wanted you to watch, baby brother," he says, looking at me across the table. "It'll be like old times." He grins when I just look at him with black eyes.

He used to make me watch. I fucking hated him for it, despised him because I got off on it. I was just a kid, but I didn't even care if he hurt them. That's how fucked up our family was. *Still is.*

"I'm going to destroy you," I say softly.

Behind me, there's the light step of someone approaching quickly, and then the feel of cool metal at the back of my head. My brother's grin widens. "Maybe not today, eh? Now sit the fuck down, Kardinal, and enjoy the entertainment with your meal." His gaze flicks to Viola whose hand is shaking as she holds the glass stem of the wine glass. Blood oozes from her palms. She must have cut herself. "And you, what the fuck are you doing with that? You little bitch. Drop it or I'll blow a hole in his fucking head."

Viola hisses but drops the glass.

Whoever is behind me, my vote is on the heavy who escorted me in here, shoves the end of the gun into my head. "You were told to sit."

I sit, reluctantly, hands gripping the leather seat while Kristian drags Viola up by her hair and forces her back down onto the glass table, into the mess of red wine and shards all over it. She kicks and bites, but Kristian doesn't fucking care. He laughs as she fights him, and all I can do is watch in slow fucking motion.

NINETEEN

VIOLA

KRISTIAN FORCES me onto the table using my broken wrist against me, finally pinning both of my arms over my head.

I kick, scream, and bite.

But he just laughs. I'm not strong enough to fight him even on a good day. He knows it. I've always known it. That's why I saved those painkillers. For this moment. But the drugs I put in his wine when he wasn't looking haven't taken effect yet. I only had a tight window to do it while he was distracted with Dino. There hasn't been enough time for them to kick in. Thirty minutes was all I needed. *Thirty fucking minutes.*

There was a small chance that it would work. I was hoping he'd at least wait until after dinner to try it on.

Laughing, Kristian uses the blade of the knife to cut the dress away. Adrenaline races through my veins. I'm not wearing any underwear because he took that when he brought the dress to the room. The last time I was used like this was a long time ago. I promised myself it would not happen again.

Not like this.

The dress falls off, the material peeling away like the petals of a wilted flower. But I'm not cold. I'm raging hot. *I'm fucking fire.* I snarl at Kristian as he moves the blade between my legs. The metal burns as he runs the edge against my skin, and slices over the top of my thigh.

"You missed several major arteries," I say with a hiss.

"Of course, I want you alive," he chuckles. He looks over at Dino. "Is this how she likes it baby brother?" he asks, bringing the knife to his lips to taste my blood.

"You fucking bastard," Dino says.

"You were always coming home with cuts and bites. I always wondered what little bitch had her claws in you." He looks down at me. "Now I know." He touches the tip of the blade at my entrance.

"Do it," I spit at him.

Wrenching my arms higher, making me growl like an animal, he grins. "Nah, I'll split you in half after I fuck you. I want you to enjoy it first."

"Your penis is the size of my little finger. How'd you expect me to enjoy that?" I say.

He just laughs. "Liar, liar, pussy on fire," he says, putting down the knife, running a heavy hand between my legs, and pulling his dick out of his pants.

I look away toward Dino who is watching with hell burning in his eyes, hands white knuckling around the base of his chair.

Kristian leans close, the heaviness of him forcing the air from my chest, the scent of him too much like Dino. His breath is hot on my neck as he whispers. "My brother won't want you after I'm finished with you. No one will. This will be the last cock you'll ever get to feel."

"I feel nothing," I say scornfully.

I don't move or scream or do anything. I just look at Dino and let everything else fall away.

Have I taught you nothing?

Dante's remark is loud inside my head. I only just hear Kristian's grunt as he shoves himself inside me.

Now. Goddamn it V, sweep.

I jerk my hips up and wrap my legs around his torso, squeezing as hard as I can. He groans as the air leaves his lungs, and he tries to move back but he can't.

I shake my head. "I've got you, you fucker. You're going nowhere," I snarl.

"Why would I want to go anywhere?" he grins, suddenly relaxing and thrusting deeper, tearing into me with the force he uses.

I almost lose my grip. Almost.

Fucking hell, V. What are you waiting for?

Kristian smirks and begins to rut, but I lock my ankles and pull up my thighs making the space between my legs as small as possible. Eyes narrowing, he stops moving, mostly because I'm preventing him. He laughs and tries again, but all I do is squeeze. It's not a sweep but it'll do.

"That's not nice." He glares, brow furrowed as he tries to extract himself.

"What? Is this not what you wanted?" I sneer, putting all my strength into bringing my thighs together.

Until I'm crushing him.

Panic reaches his eyes. The fun part is watching his eyes bulge out and his face turn red when he realizes he can't breathe. The downside is that I can still feel his cock inside me. *Don't think about that now. It's not worth thinking about.*

He snarls and smashes my face with his fist. Pain explodes in my mouth. A coppery taste fills it. But I don't break my hold. I've been trained not to. Unless he knocks me out, I'm not letting go.

Tighter.

There's a crack as I break a couple of his ribs.

"You…fucking….bitch," he gasps, slamming his fist into me again. He only gets the side of my head because I turn at the last minute. Stars burst across my vision even so. I just laugh, especially when he claws at my legs and on the table. He's trying to find the knife he dropped. *Too late.* I already have it.

Using everything I've got, I spit out a mouthful of blood, grip the hilt of the blade, and wrench myself up to ram steel into his fucking neck…

"No! Don't!" A voice shouts across the room.

I jerk my head to Dino, and I have a split second to choose. *Save Dino, or kill his fucking shit for brains brother who has his dick still inside me?*

It's not even a decision.

I hurl the knife at the guy holding the gun to Dino's head about to pull the trigger. Then I ram my fingers into Kristian's throat, so he slumps forward choking. Both men go down hard.

I don't want to feel Kristian's tiny dick inside me anymore, so I kick him backward and he falls to the floor on his knees, trousers hanging halfway down his thighs, hands pawing at his throat.

Pathetic.

I get down off the table, ignoring the raw feeling of my body, and the slice of pain through my busted lip. I'm surprisingly calm and detached, but there's a tremble in my body and my legs don't feel like they're mine.

"Viola!"

I look at Dino darkly as he comes over, yanking the jacket off his back. "Why did you stop me?" I hiss.

"He was assaulting you!" Dino exclaims, placing the jacket around my shaking shoulders, eyeing Kristian who is still coughing his guts up on the floor. In his hand is the gun Kristian's man was holding.

"All the more reason to fucking gut him then," I say, teeth chattering.

Yes, chattering. I'm cold now. Freezing. I'm so fucking sick of not being able to control my own body. I hug the jacket closer. The material is soft and smells of Dino. I don't miss him reaching for me, but he stops in time.

Don't fucking touch me.

"Fucking bitch," Kristian gasps from the floor.

Dino points the gun at him. "Stay put or I'll blow your

fucking brains out," he says. But he doesn't. He's back looking at me like I might break. "Viola, are you alright? Fuck, you're bleeding."

I drop my gaze to my thigh where Kristian cut me. It's not a deep cut. It doesn't even hurt anymore. *Nothing hurts. I'm just cold.*

"I'm fine. Just shoot him already so we can leave," I say, grabbing a napkin off the table and pressing it to my thigh.

"Kards won't kill me. I'm the only family he has left," Kristian says, breathing hard as he looks between the both of us. He focuses in on Dino. "Isn't that right, little brother?"

"Screw family," Dino growls, re-aiming the gun at his brother's head.

"Then how about this. If I don't check in with Griffin, Jude dies."

Dino glares at Kristian, but he looks conflicted.

"He's bluffing," I say.

Dino's gaze switches to me. "You know that for certain?"

"He had Griffin's niece hostage," I shrug.

Dino frowns. "I need to think. And we need to get you checked out. He just fucking raped you."

"Yes, I know. I was there," I snap at him. "Just give it to me. Give me the gun."

Dino's face hardens into rigid stone. "No, I'm getting you out of here. You're still in shock."

Kristian laughs which starts another coughing fit.

Shock? I start to laugh too because what else can I do? And once I start, I can't fucking stop.

Dino shakes his head and tries to bring me into his arms, but I push him away. I'm not ready. Not after that violation. If he touches me too soon, I might just grab that gun and shoot all the fucking men in the room, Dino included.

"Fine, then let's go. I desperately need a fucking shower."

"Wait," Dino says. He raises the gun to his brother's head. "Where is the controller for the tracker?"

Kristian smiles and pulls it out of his pocket. Dino takes it from him and switches it off. The tracker on my ankle makes a beeping noise and then falls off.

There's no car waiting for us when we get outside. I'm wearing Dino's jacket and little else when he flags a black hackney cab down. I refuse to go to the hospital, so Dino tells the driver to take us home.

Home.

Feels like so long ago it was the four of us in the frat house.

"What happened to the others?" I ask as Dino exhales after listening to a voicemail.

He shakes his head. "They got ambushed by Griffin's men. Somehow, they knew we'd be coming and where we'd be. They're fine. They managed to escape but we can't go home. They know where the frat house is. We're not safe there."

"Then where?" The chill is beginning to seep into my bones. My teeth start chattering again.

"They've sent Quinn the coordinates. I'm to call her as soon as I've got you out. Fuck you're turning blue. Here." He starts to take off his shirt.

"No, just get me somewhere I can get clean," I say.

Dino sighs and digs in his pocket for a tissue. "Your mouth is starting to bleed again," he says. I take it and dab at my lip because the cab driver is looking at us in the rearview mirror.

"What you fucking looking at?" Dino bites out at him.

"Nothing, mate. I didn't see a thing."

"Dino," I say, getting his attention back. "Where are we going?"

Dino finally relents and calls Quinn, and she sends him the details of the safe location Dante has secured for us.

He frowns as soon as he gets the address.

"What is it?" I ask.

"Fucking crazy if you ask me..." He turns his screen so I can see what's on it.

Sacré-Cœur Preparatory School
Whitechapel
London

After the driver drops us off at the main road, I leave Dino to pay him a huge tip, and walk up the long driveway to the school.

With the millions in his offshore account, Dante, according to Quinn when I made Dino call her back, went ahead and bought the buildings of Sacred Heart using a shell company he owns after the school had permanently closed. He never told me that he did that, but I guess I never asked.

Why the hell would a grown-ass man want a school?

I wait until I'm inside the building to ask him that to his face. Dante and Lorcan are sitting inside the teacher's lounge when I enter it. Well, Dante is. Lorcan is standing outside the courtyard window on his phone talking animatedly. He hasn't seen me yet.

"This is a step up from a cabin in the woods, D," I say as soon as he looks up. My eyes flick to the gaping hole in his shoulder. He's been shot.

"You made it," Dante says, jaw clenched as he takes me in. "Where are your fucking clothes?"

"Quinn's bringing some over," I say, clutching Dino's jacket around me as I stalk over to inspect Dante's wound. It's not too serious. I let out a breath. "You'll live."

"Glad to hear it. Will you?"

"Just a bruised lip, a broken wrist, and a sore head. Why this place?" I ask him, ignoring his real question because I'm not ready for it, roving my eyes over the chintzy sofas and the dark wood paneling on the walls.

What just happened is going into a dark pit in the depths of my psyche like everything else, to be dealt with a lot later.

"It's the last place anyone, including your father, would look for us," Dante says.

I nod but furrow my brow, glancing back at the guy I grew up with. "That's why you bought it?" *I know nothing about this man.*

"No. I bought it because after you killed the headmaster, it was dirt cheap." He smirks. "And I always wanted to run an assassin school."

I stare at him until I realize he's fucking with me.

I punch him in the shoulder.

"Goddamnit, V." He winces.

"Don't fuck with me." I glare until he holds up a hand.

"Fine, fine." He gives a slight chuckle. "Besides being a hitman, I also flip property. And I'm going to make a killing turning this place into apartments." I always wanted to know what Dante does besides slaughter people. Now I know. It seems too mundane.

His blue eyes run up and down the length of me. There's an expression of concern.

"What?" I ask.

"You're off your game." His eyes narrow as he cocks his head. "What happened?"

I shake my head. *No. I'm not going there.* Whatever happened in that house with Kristian stays in the fucking dark pit until I kill him.

"I'm fine," I lie as the door opens and Dino bursts in with Quinn.

"Oh my fucking god," she exclaims as she storms over. She takes one look at me and shoots an evil eye at Dante as though it's his fault, and then escorts me down the hallway to the girls' locker room where she orders me to shower and change.

I don't try to fight her.

I'm done fighting for a little while.

In actual fact, I might be done, period.

After I skin Kristian alive and cook his genitals while he watches.

TWENTY

VIOLA

THE BOYS TIPTOE around me for a few days. I don't know what they think I'm going to do, but it's like I'm on death row and there's a ticking clock over my head counting down until the end of fucking time.

We take up quarters in the boarding house part of the school. Most of the school body were day students, but a small number actually lived here. Out of the six apartments with three double bedrooms each, we take the top floor which is the biggest and the most lavish. Quinn gets her own room and so do I. The boys take turns sleeping on the sofa or patrolling campus like we're in some kind of military base.

Most nights I wake up sweating, pawing at the duvet, my throat hoarse from screaming. And all four of my newfound housemates come running in to check on me. Usually, Dante first. Then the boys and Quinn. Then I tell them all to fuck off and leave me alone.

"That wasn't the first time that's happened," I say to Dino when he asks me for the hundredth time if I'm okay after bringing me a cup of coffee. I'm sitting in a chair, watching Quinn work a week after we arrived.

Quinn has turned the warden's office on the ground floor of the boarding house into her own personal computer lab, complete with all her equipment she brought with her. She's trying to find Rebecca.

I can't do fuck all until I know she's safe.

"It doesn't work like that, and you know it," Quinn says after Dino leaves sharpish.

I shoot her a look. "I'm not some delicate flower," I say.

"Oh, I know that." Quinn scowls. Her hair is tied back into a ponytail and her face is free of makeup. She's not a girl to fuss over her looks, but she manages to pull it off effortlessly anyway. It's one of the things I enjoy about her. "But PTSD can affect everyone. It doesn't discriminate."

I give her a blank look before putting my cup on the desk. "I'm going for a run."

"Just tell me how you feel, and then you can go."

"I feel fine," I say.

She raises both brows. "Do you? Because last I checked you were beaten up and raped. There's nothing wrong in taking the time to heal."

I give her a look. "How can I take time to heal when Rebecca is still missing?"

"She's your mother. She will understand. It's her job to protect you, not the other way around."

"My mother understands fuck all, hence the reason for her being in a mental institute all my adult fucking life," I say acidly.

"What happened to you, V? The last time I saw you, you were starting to let others in. A major breakthrough. And now you've regressed back into a cold-blooded killer, I'm worried. You're spending too much time with Dante, and not enough with those who care about you."

Her words are starting to annoy me. I get to my feet. "Is that all?" I ask her, letting her see the 'I don't give a shit' attitude in my eyes.

"Not yet. He's no good for you, V. He's an infectious disease. Every time you're around him, you become this thing that's dead inside," Quinn adds.

I give her a blank look, showing just how dead inside I can be. "Can I go now?"

Quinn stares at me and then makes a waving motion with her hand. "Go, but please think about what I've said. I miss the Viola who was falling in love."

I snort at that and walk out of Quinn's office to go for that run.

"Dante will be waiting for you in the medical bay to check on your hand," Quinn calls out as I'm closing the door behind me.

Cool air breezes through my hair, slicking the sweat on my brow. This run is what I need. Just me and the road, and my music.

I am fine.

It's not a lie. I feel like I always do, like I'm waiting for my next hit of torture and death to feel something. Except there's a shift. A subtle one. I'm falling and I can't quite catch the edge. I can't quite shake off the coldness. It's like the chill from that day never fucking left. Even though this isn't anything I haven't handled before. It hasn't happened since I made a promise to myself to never be in the same position again. Not unless I want it. The last time a guy did that to me, I bit his ear off before I shoved a knife in his gut.

He was one of my first kills.

And of course, he wasn't my last.

Adjusting my earphones, I change my route to take the long way around the school. Without students, the school is the perfect place for me. There are thousand places I can go to be alone—the boathouse for one. Even if Dante has rigged the whole place up with cameras.

I pound the pavement until I get to the walkway in the fields

167

that lead to the boys' old stomping ground. There's a huge lock on the doors of the wooden building where the boats are stored.

The boathouse itself is not locked, not anymore. But I don't go inside. I run around it until I see him sitting, waiting.

Lorcan squints as he sees me coming down the jetty. It's become a morning ritual for us to meet here and sit close to the lake. Lorcan doesn't sneak into my room at night like he used to, so this is what we do now.

"Any word on Griffin?" I ask him, inhaling hard while I catch my breath.

Lorcan tugs his headphones off, shaking his head. "The bastard has gone underground. If what Lily said was true, Kristian was using Pascal to keep Griffin in check which means he could be swayed to our side."

"He might know where my mother is," I say.

Lorcan glances up at me again and nods as I sit down next to him taking my shoes and socks off to stick my feet in the cold water. Lorcan frowns because it's mid-February. But if I'm cold inside, I may as well be cold outside too.

After a pause, Lorcan says, "He's not like you and me, you know."

"Who?" I say, even though I know very well who he means.

"Dino. Killing doesn't come easy for him. You need to stop punishing him."

I slide my gaze to him. "I thought that's what you were doing?"

Lorcan's jaw tightens as he stares at the lake. The apartments aren't soundproof. I've heard the disagreements between the two of them over the last few days. Lorcan blames Dino for what happened to me. It's all fucked up and no one has any balls to accept it and move on.

"I'm not going to break," I say out loud. *Because I'm already broken. And I have been for a very long time.*

"No, but Sinner might."

"What do you mean?"

"Killing his brother in front of him. Don't do it. For the love of all things fucked up, keep him from ever seeing that. He saw his father murdered and butchered in front of him, and it broke him."

"We've all seen dark things," I say.

Lorcan snorts. "Not all of us can be shit hot assassins."

"Fine, I get it. Keep Dino away from the darkness."

After a pause, Lorcan speaks again. "How long are we staying here?"

"I don't understand the question," I say. And I don't. We have nowhere else to go.

Lorcan sighs and scrubs his face with his hand, then he looks at me. "We're really staying here? At our old school? With Psycho fucking Charlie calling the shots."

I frown at him. I thought he was over this.

"I don't trust him," he adds. "None of us do."

He means Dante. "Well I do, so fucking get used to it," I say, teeth gritted. I go to grab my shoes and socks and stand up but he grabs my hand.

His green eyes are dark and tortured as he regards me. "You know I fucking miss you," he says.

With a sigh, I sit down again. I don't put my feet in the water. There's only so much cold you can take. He eyes the space between us. It's not enough he can't reach over and touch me, but I can tell he's hesitating. Desire clouds his face as he takes in the running gear I'm wearing.

This treating me like glass has to stop.

I lean over suddenly and press my lips to his. He doesn't move at first. And then he does, gently taking me in his arms. His fingers curl in my hair as he brings me close.

I kiss him harder, closing my teeth on his soft lips, making him growl. He smells of woody cologne and windswept lakes. He tastes of something I've been missing and didn't know I'd lost. My fingers entwine in his hair until they're thick with it, then I break the kiss and snatch his head back.

He gives a sharp intake of breath.

"Stop treating me like I'm dead," I say coolly.

"Only if you talk to someone about what fucking happened," he says, eyes narrowed. "It doesn't have to be me. Quinn or…"

"No," I say to him, shaking my head. "We're not doing this."

"The other girls at—"

"I said no." I grab my things and walk off before he can finish the rest of the sentence.

I don't need or want his pity. He was about to say something about the girls at his school and how fucked they were when they came back from whatever dark place they agreed to go. I'm not one of his schoolgirls. I'm a killer. And if I have to remind him and Dino of that, then so be it.

I stop to put my shoes and socks back on, and stalk away from the boathouse, breaking out into a run once I get to the path. My feet are wet and frozen in my trainers, but I don't care. I wait until I'm in the middle of the woods about a mile away before losing my restraint. I stop running and scream as loud as I can, clenching my fists into tight balls. Then I kick a tree over and over at the base.

My other wrist hasn't healed yet, so I feel the throb of pain through the splint Dante applied, bringing me back to my senses.

I'm so over this!

TWENTY-ONE

VIOLA

BACK AT THE MAIN CAMPUS, Dante is indeed waiting for me in the medical bay. He cocks a brow but doesn't say a word as I hop onto the exam bed like I have been doing every day since we got here.

"I want you in the gym tomorrow," he says, like we're back in training and he has the right to order me about.

"My wrist hasn't healed."

"Then you'll work the rest of your body until it has," he says, checking the splint is still applied correctly.

"When did you become a doctor again?" I say flippantly.

He raises a brow and carries on checking me over. My lip has all but healed and the cut on my thigh has crusted over nicely. I was lucky. So was Dante. His gunshot wound turned out to be a bullet that went straight through and did minimal damage. He didn't need too many stitches.

Dante has medical training, that's obvious. I made a joke. But he's patched me up professionally one too many times too for it to be a fluke. And watching Dante fish bullets out of his own body, as well as sew himself back up, tells me once again I know hardly anything about him. We grew up together, but there was a period of his life when he left, and I have no idea what he did in that time.

I don't blame him for leaving. Although, it was after he left that everything went to shit. My mother got worse. Adrien brought me to his parties and made me do things I still have nightmares about today. I want to blame Dante for leaving me. But if anyone should be blamed, it's Adrien. He gave me to Kristian, just like he gave me to all those other men.

Lorcan and Quinn are wrong. Dante has always protected me, and in the best way possible—by teaching me to protect myself.

"Okay, tell me what's on your mind before you draw blood," he asks, curtailing my trip through memory lane.

I look down to see my nails digging into Dante's forearm. He raises both brows at me but doesn't move his arm until I let him go.

"Why the hell are we waiting here?" I ask. After what Lorcan said, I need to know.

Dante walks over to the counter and picks up a black book with Chinese symbols on it. He tosses it onto my lap. "Here, read this."

"Really? You want me to read a book?"

"Honestly, you don't read enough."

I slit my eyes at him, then exhale as I pick up the damned book. "The Art of War," I read out loud.

"Chapter five," Dante says with a nod.

I flip to chapter five, humoring him. "Tactical Dispositions." I roll my eyes. This isn't some military attack we're planning.

"Just fucking read it and stop whining," he says, a slight twitch to his lips.

Trust Dante to make this into a fucking learning experience. I take the book and get off the bed.

"V," Dante says softly as I start to walk out of the room.

I turn around and suddenly he's there, seizing me by the neck and pulling me to him. I throw the book at him, expecting an attack, but all he does is kiss me.

His mouth is soft, but his kiss is hard and unyielding. He pushes me up against the wall and devours me against it until I'm no longer capable of breathing.

I'm kissing Dante.

My mind can't comprehend it, but I don't push him away. My body reacts, wrapping itself around him as he traps me between him and the cool white tiles. He smells like he always has….

Of fire and gasoline. Of death and darkness.

The lamp on the desk next to us falls with a clatter as we move on to it.

As his hands, calloused and rough, glide under my running top to grab my breasts, thumbs teasing over my nipples. I bite down on his tongue as it plunges inside me and swirls all the non-existent emotions up so they come roaring to the surface.

Breathing hard, he pulls back slightly, eyes dark. "I'm not one of your schoolboys," he says.

"You don't like the taste of blood?" I say, my lips still inches from his. The heat that pooled in my groin when Lorcan kissed me has already ignited with molten fury. I run my hands over his chest, feeling the scar where I bit him months ago.

"That's not what I'm saying. This is not a casual fuck."

Fuck? My eyes narrow at his words, pulse thudding in my ears. "What is this then?"

"You're mine," he says. "You always have been."

"And you've only just realized it now?"

"I've only just realized this is what you need," he scoffs, dragging a hand through my hair until the roots burn. And then he kisses me again.

He's right. I need him to burn the memory of Kristian away.

I need Dante to make me his.

As if reading my thoughts, he kisses down my neck and bites me, branding my neck and shoulder with a mark of his own. Pain mixed with pleasure sweeps through my whole body. He hauls

175

down the front of my jogging bottoms and dips a hand between my legs, expertly eliciting a soft moan from my lips. The feel of him touching me is fire. I'm in the middle of it. Consumed by it.

"I'm going to take the pain away," he says.

"Mmm," is all I can say in response. I can't speak. I can't move. I'm frozen in place.

Like a rabbit caught in fucking headlights.

Taking that as a yes, he drops between my legs, pulling down my joggers and thong. Eyes closed, head tilted back, I immerse myself in his attention. Dante continues to drag his lips over my body until he sweeps a hot tongue between my folds. Desperate pleasure explodes through me. I grab fistfuls of his long hair, hungry for more.

When I don't feel him again, I glance down. Dante is watching me, icy blue eyes filled with need, a dark smile on his lips.

"I've waited a long time to do this," he says.

"Don't stop," I demand.

"Oh, I'm not. This is just what you need." he says, going back to licking me out, thrusting deeper every time, sucking at my clit until I can do nothing but ride the wave of need erupting at my core. When I'm panting and dripping for him, he pushes me back on the table and takes off his shirt. Flashbacks of Kristian tear through my mind, but then Dante's scent overrides all that as he leans over me to drop burning kisses onto my aching skin, pulling my sports clothes off until I'm naked and completely at his mercy.

Suddenly, he pulls back, looking down on me intently, eyes never once leaving mine. He likes to take his time. Like an apex predator with his prey.

Only I'm the prey.

A shiver runs up and down my spine. Although, I'm no longer cold. I'm burning a fever just having him look at me like I've always wanted him to.

He unbuttons the fly of his jeans, unveiling his cock for me. I let my gaze fall to it. It's beautiful...*and it's all fucking mine*. I sit up and seal my mouth to his, tasting my own juices as my hand reaches to wrap around his shaft. It's velvet soft and rock hard in my hands. I grip him hard and then tease him with my nails. My mouth waters at the thought of running my tongue along the length and over the tip, tasting him.

I lick my lips.

I push him back and move off the desk, still kissing him. Then I drop in front of him. Never would I have ever thought I'd be in this position—on my knees about to take Dante's thick cock in my mouth. The thought exhilarates me, releases me. It's like I'm floating above all the noise in my head. Nothing makes sense anymore but this moment. After all, I've waited my whole life for it.

As he watches me with devilish eyes, I part my lips and slide his length all the way to the back of my throat. I groan and close my eyes when he doesn't quite make it all the way in. Tasting him, sweet desire mixed with sultry darkness, I'm lost and found all at once.

"Fucking hell, V," Dante says in a low, guttural voice, almost a growl. He grabs me by my hair, straining at my delay. His words and fingers running through my hair and over my scalp, pulling tight, wake me out of my stupor. I move my mouth over his delicious cock, sucking the essence of him down, breathing in the scent of him. He's ash and death, and everything I've ever known.

He growls again and grips my head hard, angling it so he can thrust deeper. He wants control so I let him take it. I open my soul to him and let him fuck my mouth savagely, using me, owning me, until I'm close to choking. I'm slick with desire when he finally pulls out.

He drags me up and pushes me back onto the desk.

"That was fucking heaven," he says as he drops his head to mine and brutally kisses me full on the lips. "But now you're mine."

Hearing him curse has me moaning into his mouth. I'm desperate for him, greedy, as he breaks the kiss.

"Fuck me on the desk," I plead. I need him to destroy the

ghost of Kristian that still haunts me. He needs to take me in the same position and burn that fucking memory to ashes.

His brow furrows but he nods and holds me down on the desk, pressing his cock between my legs as I open them. I let out a feral sound as he rubs against me. At last, I feel the tip slide in. But not all the way. He stops, making me wait. I'm soaked, aching all over, begging to be filled. I'm practically shaking.

And he fucking stopped.

I stare up into his icy blue eyes, and I have no idea why he's not fucking me yet. But I'm done waiting. I never use my mouth like that. Blow jobs—I just don't. But Dante is different. As soon as I saw his perfect length, I longed to taste him. And now I need him to fuck me with that perfection. I gave. Now he needs to take. As if reading my thoughts, Dante smirks. I scowl and try to wrap my legs around him to nestle closer, but he pushes me back down.

"Just fuck me already," I hiss as I look up from where I'm lying on the desk.

"I'll fuck you when I'm good and ready," he says smoothly, pushing inside me a little more. Still not all the way. I dig my nails into his arms and glare into his eyes. He chuckles, as though he knows how much this is killing me.

"Tell me how much you want this," he says, head cocked.

"I need it. I need you."

He smiles devilishly, and drives his hips forward, filling me up, stretching me completely. The soreness that was there from before, and the size of him shoving deeply in, is eased by how dripping wet I am for him. Still, I groan loudly, mouth open and eyes wide, which just makes him fuck me again twice as hard.

"You're going too slow," I breathe out.

He shakes his head. "No, this is how I want to take you. I want to enjoy every second of you, V."

Then he fucks me. *Slowly.*

The pace is damn near brutal.

I clench around him, eyes open the entire time, burning the vision of Dante fucking me into my brain. The feeling of him stretching me, thrusting deeper, has my heart hammering in my chest. Every moan I give off makes his thrust a little harder. Every gasp I make, has me growling with pleasure. Dante watches, amused the whole fucking time.

"What's so funny?" I gasp.

"You. I'm enjoying making you squirm over my cock. You're pretty fucking perfect." He slams into me roughly on the word perfect.

The pleasure has wrapped around my core, tightening every time he drives into me. When his hand holding me down moves to squeeze my breast, the other one strokes around my clit, and I can no longer hold back.

I come hard, shuddering around him.

My release is earth shattering and long over fucking due. Then I come again, harder this time as he thrusts into me relentlessly, while I say his name like a prayer on my lips. Finally, he pulls out and coats my stomach and chest with his cum, the whole time watching me with an intense gaze full of lust and dark promises.

I'm panting, covered in him. It runs down my stomach as he drags me up to claim my mouth with his. I melt against him, shaking and satisfied both at once.

Dante was right. This was what I needed.

He was what I needed.

"How did you know?" I ask, wiping myself down with some of the medical bed sheets before dressing. There's a shower in the medical bay, but I prefer to shower in my own room alone. Not that I would expect Dante to jump in with me. I don't know what this is between us, but I don't need to know. I was broken, or close to it. I still am, but at least I've chased the demons in my head away for a while.

Dante gives me a look, corner of his lips twitching. Then he comes over and puts his arms around me. I'm not expecting him to, and it makes me tense. "Because I know you, V. I've known you my whole life," he says, looking down at me. He takes me by the chin and draws my face up to look at him. "And because you've always been mine."

I don't know what to say to that, so I just give a light shove, and gather my hoodie off the chair, and stalk toward the exit.

I don't know what to think anymore. It's a fucking mess inside my head, even if my body is less rebellious now it's found some sweetness in hell.

"Don't forget. Training tomorrow," Dante calls out.

I give him the finger and walk out the room.

TWENTY-TWO

DANTE

VIOLA IS ABSOLUTELY PERFECT.

She always has been. There's a reason I kept her around. I stalked her to hell and back. I trained her and taught her everything she knows. Then I let her go. But she came back, because deep down she knows she's mine.

All mine.

I watch her walk out of the treatment room and allow the corners of my mouth to curl up. Fucking her just now was not my intention. I usually like to draw things out. I'm a long game kind of guy, but suddenly I just couldn't hold back. Her pain was palatable. She was desperate. I could taste her darkness on her lips and that was all it took.

I don't regret moving so soon. I would do it all over again, and I will. I promise her that. I meant it when I said I wasn't just another one of her schoolboys. I will have her again, and when I do, she'll beg me to destroy her. The taste of her skin, the sound of her breathy moans as her pink lips made the perfect O, even the feel of her around my cock.

Goddamn, V. What have you done to me? I'm already hard just thinking about thrusting into her lithe body again, making it undeniably mine.

But I *need* to focus.

I should have stayed away from her. I really should have. But V is an addiction. One I've already accepted. And like everything involving V, this addiction complicates things. Women are for fucking. I enjoy them, but I much prefer to work. What happens when your work becomes the woman you care about? Everything falls down. Messy and unpredictable are things I stay away from.

But I can't stay away from V.

After she's gone, I clean up and hit the gym. I don't see Viola for the rest of the day. When I get back to the boarding house, I find her with Quinn trying to decipher some of her father's emails after Quinn has hacked into his system. I snort when she tells me. She asks me why and I explain. Her father is careful. He might be someone I despise, but he's not going to leave all his plans in the open where any old hack can find them.

Quinn shoots me another hateful look, so I leave them to it. Quinn has had it in for me since I tied her to a chair and threatened to kill her. It wasn't personal. It was business. I actually don't mind the girl.

Still, I'm not here to make friends.

I'm here for V, and her alone.

I owe her that.

Viola turns up the next day for training in the gym at 7 a.m. sharp. I'm a little surprised to see Duke with her, but I acknowledge him with a nod. We take turns sparring one on one. I go with V first, who is rusty as hell. I get her on her back a few times, despite my shoulder, earning daggered looks from her boyfriend. I ignore him, enjoying the way her body yields to mine. The look on her face is indignant, but also filled with desire. Lips parted, and eyes half-lidded and alluring.

It's exactly what I want to see.

Over the years, I've toyed with making V mine completely, but I've never gone through with it for all sorts of reasons. Maybe I shouldn't have waited. Then again, I'm a patient man. I would wait for Viola until the last second, just to enjoy the chase.

"Is this all you've got?" she sneers as I get her on her back again in a choke hold with my weight to one side so she can't bridge her back or buck me off.

"I can do this all night," I say, tightening my grip, looking into those brown eyes of hers.

"Are you both fucking serious?"

We both glance to the side to see Duke staring down at us. I smirk at him and let V up, offering a hand to her so she can climb to her feet. Her left wrist is still healing so I want to give her as much support as possible.

Duke scowls at me and takes V's place on the mat. He's not bad at grappling, and a few times he gets me in a hold even though he can't seem to keep me there. The way he moves suggests he's trained before. I'm impressed, and that takes a lot.

V snorts and rolls her eyes as she watches us. She's curious as to who is better. She's also turned on. I can see in the way her chest rises, her irises become large, and she bites her lower lip. When I get her boyfriend on the mat again, flat on his back, she exhales and moistens them.

Interesting.

She still has feelings for him.

At the end of the session, I take her aside. Duke gives me a dark look, but he gets the message and leaves.

"If you want him, I'm fine with that," I say, keeping my voice neutral after he's gone.

Her eyes blaze as she scowls. "What the fuck? Are you giving me permission now? I fuck who I like, D. You don't own me."

I let my mouth curl up as I take her in. Hair snatched back in a ponytail, eyes stormy, mouth sulky and petulant. Right now, she's one hundred percent fuckable.

I place my hand around her delicate neck and pull her to me, tasting the salty sweat on her lips. She smells earthy and fragrant at the same time.

When I release her, she's staring at me with a mix of lust and annoyance.

"Of course I own you. Do as I say and maybe I'll fuck you again."

She glares and I chuckle. The kitten is adorable when she shows her claws. I push her away and walk toward the men's changing room. My luck is severely lacking when Duke is waiting when I come out of the shower.

He's in his preppy clothes, leaning against the lockers. It takes everything not to roll my eyes. It wouldn't do to upset the boy. I turn around and open my locker.

"I think we need to sort this out," he says, burning a hole into the back of my head.

I look over my shoulder at him while I dry off and put on a change of clothes.

"Sure," I say. If it makes him feel better to talk, I'm not going to stop him.

He rubs his chin as he steps forward, and then exhales sharply, an unamused smile on his face. "This is fucking harder than I thought."

I cross my arms. "I'm listening."

He looks at me and shrugs. "I thought you'd be a dick and you are." I raise both brows. After a few seconds, he carries on. "But Viola wants you around and I respect her decision, even if I want to gut you where you stand half the fucking time. You tried to kill my sister but you're a hired psycho fuck and you were just doing your job, so I'm giving you the benefit of the doubt. Especially since you saved Viola more times that I can count."

"Right," I say. "Is that it?"

Duke nods, corners of his mouth turned down. "Pretty much. Just don't fucking hurt her."

"Or?"

His eyes narrow. "Or I'll carve you into tiny pieces and feed you to the fucking ducks." He gives me one last glare, and then shoves his hands in his pockets and walks out.

Vice is up next, accosting me in the kitchen. He glares at me as he walks in. "What did you do to her?"

I give him a look that I reserve from my targets just before I blow their brains out. Vice suddenly looks nervous, but I'll give him his due, he doesn't back down or leave me alone. After half a minute, he crosses his arms.

I let out a sigh and go back to pouring myself a glass of orange juice. "We had sex," do you have a problem with that?"

"Fucking what now?" He pales visibly, shaking his head. "Viola would never…" He stops, unfolds his arms, and runs a hand through his hair, then he looks at me. "You know she was recently sexually assaulted by my brother right?"

I raise a brow at him. "The brother you allowed to live? Yes, I know about that, and I eased her pain." I step close, letting him see the darkness within me that would snap his neck without a second thought. Unlike Duke, Vice is weak, and he knows it. "What did *you* do to take her suffering away? Absolutely fuck all."

He glares at me. "She's not like you. Killing won't solve this."

I cock my head and smirk. "Boy, V is exactly like me. And trust me, killing to her is everything. If you don't know that by now, you soon will."

The effect is spoiled by me holding a glass of orange juice, so I do the only thing that comes naturally—I take a sip and leave the room.

Fucking schoolboys.

The fact that I'm angry enough to curse is telling in itself. I need something to focus on before I unravel. I've only ever let my demon take control once. Just once.

And it was enough.

I take my orange juice and head to see Quinn in her makeshift office.

"Any news on Griffin?"

She looks up, eyes darkening when she sees me. "He's gone dark. The only possible lead I have is that his niece, Pascal Havemeyer was picked up at 7a.m. this morning outside her house."

"Are we tracking her?"

She raises a brow. "Are you insulting my intelligence now?"

"Is that a yes?"

She scowls. "That's a yes. I've been tracking her all morning. She's at Billingsgate Market. My hunch is Griffin is there too."

I nod at her. "Then we go and find him."

"We?" Says Viola stepping into the room. "You mean the both of us, right?"

"I wouldn't have it any other way," I say.

Ten minutes later, we're on the road. Viola won't stop fiddling with the radio. It's distracting but she is in her very nature *distracting*. I shouldn't question what I'm doing, moving our relationship forward to the level it's at. What's done is done. But I have to consider my timing. It's made my life difficult in a very short space of time. *School boys aside.*

"Talk to me, V," I say, because I know there's something on her mind. "What is it you want to tell me?" Viola only has ADHD when she can't quite express how she feels. Trying to get her to sit still will be impossible, unless I drag it out of her.

She glances at me and scowls. "How do you do that?"

"Do what?" I ask her.

"Get inside my head."

I shrug. "Training, now what is it? You've been skittish since you got here."

After a few seconds, she sighs. "When we were at Adrien's estate, I found a file on you in his office."

She's watching me in the darkened interior of the car, waiting to see how I'll react. Adrien having files on me isn't new. And I've seen what's inside a few because he's shown me them. Adrien likes to have knowledge over people as power. It's how he works. Whereas I just want the money.

I wait Viola out because there's more than she's letting on.

"Did you know your mother was Adrien's childhood sweetheart, but she ran away from him on their wedding day?"

"I didn't know that," I say carefully.

"When you were just a toddler, Adrien tracked her down. He killed her and her lover and then took you for his own. There was a birth certificate in the file and newspaper clippings."

"Where's this file?"

"I took a picture of it with Dino's phone, but the actual file is back at the estate."

I nod, taking in her words as much as I can right now.

After a minute of silence, V speaks up. "I was waiting for the right moment to tell you," she says.

"Now probably wasn't the right time," I say. "We need to concentrate on what's happening now." I shoot a glance over to her as she rolls her eyes.

"Fine," she says.

"You need to make a deal with Griffin. Offer him part of Adrien's empire," I say.

"Fuck no," she snorts.

I glance at her and shake my head. "Someone ratted us out when we were at Kristian's place. My hunch is Kato did. I found the guy who they killed when we were at the casino, or the remains of him. It was your father's mark. The one he sent you to kill that night before you got distracted."

She frowns as she takes this in. "So, it wasn't one of my father's men?"

"No, which means we're an ally short. You need Griffin."

"I don't need anyone. Let them all rot in hell," she retorts.

"Fine." I'm going to have to think of another way to get Griffin on board. Viola is being extra stubborn today. "At least let me do the talking once we find him," I say with a sigh.

"Fuck talking." She snorts. "He knows where Rebecca is and if the fucker has done anything to Jude…" She stops talking.

"Jude?" I say. *Yet another boyfriend to deal with.*

She looks over at me, brushing her hair out of her eyes. "When

Kristian had me locked up, he was threatening Jude. That was why Dino didn't kill him."

"Jude can take care of himself," I say bluntly.

Her brow furrows. "No one has heard from him."

I nod at that, taking the information in. "Do you remember what I said about reducing your liabilities? You seem to be collecting them."

She scowls. "I'm not in the mood for a lecture right now, Dante."

"Then get in the mood," I say simply.

We both lapse into silence after that. It's welcome after all the talking I've had to endure. Talking is overrated.

There should be less of it.

Billingsgate fish market is closed when we get there, since it's late in the day. It makes it easier for Griffin to spot our approach. All I have to do is park up and wait. After a few minutes, one of Griffin's men walks toward the car and taps on the window. I wind it down, letting in a gust of air and the smell of fish. Griffin's guy tosses a buzzing phone through the window and onto my lap.

Viola dives for it first but I beat her to it. There's an advantage to having lightning-fast reflexes.

"There'd better be a perfectly good reason you're parked outside my market," Griffin says down the line as soon as I place it to my ear.

"Viola was the one who got Pascal out. You owe her," I say directly.

"Is that so?"

"Just tell us where Rebecca is, and we'll be on our way." Out the corner of my eye, Griffin's man is hovering. I close the window. Viola is making eyes at me. She wants me to ask about Jude. If I do that before asking about Rebecca, Griffin might use him as leverage.

"I don't know where Rebecca is," he says after a pause.

"You don't know where your men took her after they picked her up from Beckbridge House?"

"Hey, I was just doing what Adrien paid me to do. We dropped her off at his house after we collected. That was the deal." He sounds sincere so I try a different tact.

"And the Marques boy? I hear your boys are treating him like one of their own." I can't ignore Viola anymore so I place the phone on speaker so she can hear firsthand what his answer to that is.

"He's a Marques, isn't he? Albert's boy. Of course I'm looking out for him."

"That's not what Kristian said," V says sharply. "He said that all he had to do was give the order and you'd execute him." There's a dangerous glint in her eye that precedes one of her rash decisions. Her hand is on the door handle of the Mustang, ready to bolt.

I place a palm on her thigh and massage it. That startles her. I enjoy doing that a little too much.

"Kristian thinks a lot of himself, doesn't he?" Griffin says. "He had Pascal. I couldn't risk him hurting her."

"Does that mean Jude is safe?"

"As fucking houses," Griffin replies. "Just keep me out of your mess and your boy will be home in no time at all."

"You touch a fucking—"

"Done," I say, cutting Viola off before she can say anything more scathing. I switch the phone off, lower the window, and throw it out to Griffin's guy still outside the car.

Viola glances at me, eyes narrowed into slits. "I wasn't fucking finished."

"You were. Jude will survive another night, but Rebecca might not," I say. "You also need to learn to use the tools around you. Griffin happens to be a very useful one."

I don't wait to argue with V. She hasn't seen the message from Quinn yet, but I have.

I slam the car into reverse, almost knocking Griffin's guy over.

There's a bump as I drive over his foot, and he roars in pain and punches a fist through the rear side window.

"What the fuck?!" Viola exclaims, as glass shatters all over the back seat.

Jaw clenched, I shift into drive and peel around the back of the market where there's another entrance, and block Pascal Havemeyer from getting into a waiting town car.

V, for all her fucking distractions, does what I need her to without being asked. She sees the girl, shoots me a look, and then yanks open her door and drags the poor girl kicking and screaming into the passenger seat.

"See," I say, as I switch gears and accelerate us out of the market. "Goddamn useful."

TWENTY-THREE

VIOLA

QUINN IS furious with us for kidnapping Pascal, but I deal with her the same way I dealt with all the fucking drama—I let it wash over me.

My wrist aches after the stunt we pulled, but it was worth it. As soon as we got back to the school gates, an enraged Griffin called Pascal's phone. After we assured him we wouldn't hurt her, it was just to get his attention, he offered to broker a trade with Adrien. Rebecca for Pascal.

Dante stalks off somewhere into the depths of the school, so I take a moment to myself. I leave Quinn to fuss over the crying girl and go to the room I've commandeered as mine. As soon as I shut the door, I lean against it with my eyes closed. The buzzing is back. It didn't take long for it to worm its way under my skin. I didn't kill Kristian so I can only fathom it's the aftermath of that need coming back to taunt me.

There's a knock at the door.

I stay as still as possible hoping it will go away.

"Viola, we need to talk to you," says Dino.

I used to live alone. I used to relish having no one to have to talk to. And now once again, I have people who think it's fine to beat down my door and demand to talk whenever it suits them.

With a sigh, I pull away from the door and open it. Lorcan and Dino are waiting behind it for me to let them in. Actually, Lorcan doesn't wait. He strides in, followed by a hesitant Dino.

"You kidnapped a girl?" Dino hisses as soon as he sees me. The asshole has been avoiding me for the past week. He doesn't get an answer.

I shoot my eyes heavenward and shut the door so everyone can't hear. I could tell them it was Dante's idea but that would just cause conflict between them, and Lorcan was just coming round to the idea of Dante being part of whatever this is.

What is this?

I give an internal shrug to that question and stare at Lorcan. "We're just borrowing her to get leverage on Griffin. It's just until we get my mother back and we know Jude is safe."

That unsettles them. The accusation in their eyes is annoying but after letting that sink in, it's replaced with confusion. Lorcan looks confused anyway.

"Dino didn't tell you," I say to Lorcan, glancing at Dino for confirmation.

His brow furrows. "No, what didn't you fucking tell me?"

Interesting. Dino is keeping secrets now. He usually tells Lorcan everything. He glares at Dino so I continue so we can all move on. "Kristian threatened Jude. That's why Dino didn't kill him," I say.

"Griffin's boys are at St Michael's" Lorcan says, nodding.

"That's why we took his niece."

"Then we get Jude out," says Lorcan simply.

"You can do that?" I ask him.

"If he hasn't found Byron by now, then he's not going to. I'll call his lawyer tomorrow and arrange it."

I furrow my brow. "Do I want to know how?"

Lorcan rubs his chin, letting out a breath. "I don't want to call it a bribe but there are special program initiatives that he can be elected for if certain donations are made. It also helps that my father kept videotapes of everyone who has ever abused his network of underage girls."

I nod, taking it in. Good to know Duke has that reach.

"I still don't like it," says Dino. "She's just a teenager for fuck's sake."

There's another knock at the door. I roll my eyes again because what else can I do? "Come in. Everyone come in and join the fucking party."

It's Quinn. She tosses her hair as she strides in. Behind her is a timid looking Pascal who shrinks behind the tall Asian as soon as she sees me.

"You can come in too. I'm not going to bite," I snap.

Dino frowns at me and I have to dig my nails into the palm of my hand to stop myself from screaming.

Lorcan is the only one who notices, and he grabs my hand. "Use me," he says softly. "If you need to hurt someone, I'm here." I study him and after a few seconds, I nod. He knows me. I forget that we lived together for a while, and he got to know my quirks as much as I came to understand his. Lor was the only one who got that I occasionally needed an outlet.

He's not the only one, Viola. What happened between you and Dante yesterday was exactly that. D understanding you.

Dino on the other hand...The asshole is glaring at me like I killed his kitten.

Quinn too for that matter.

She throws me a dark look. "This doesn't mean I agree with what you and that psycho did, but..." She glances at Pascal, softening her features to address the girl. "Tell Viola what you told me."

Pascal stares at the floor and just when I think she's going to vomit over her shoes, she speaks. "They think I don't know but I do."

"Know what?" I say, a little too abruptly.

Pascal trembles. Immediately, I want to grab the girl and shake her.

"It's okay, Pascal. No one here will hurt you. I'll make sure of that," Quinn says. She flicks me a shitty gaze as she says it. Dino is right. There's something wrong with me.

Eventually, Pascal's eyes seek mine. They're brimming with fear. I should feel sorry for her but all I feel is contempt. "It's Lily. After we left that house, we swapped numbers and kept in touch. We were supposed to meet a few days later because Lily thought she knew where Rebecca was and wanted to check before we came to you guys, but I saw them grab her and take her."

"Who took her?" I say, keeping my voice level, trying not to be a bitch.

"I don't know, but she sent me a text." She looks at me. I confiscated her phone, but I gave it to Dino. We all wait while he fumbles around in his pocket for it. All the while, I'm using Lorcan's hand to channel my newfound anger. Although it's not new, it's old. There's just more of it now than there was. A lot more.

Dino hands it to Pascal who unlocks it, finds the message, and hands it back to Dino. He swears under his breath when he reads it.

He passes it to me.

It's a text message from Lily alright, sent late last night.

I'm sending this before they take my phone. I'm okay. With Aunty Rebecca. Send help to that place I told you. I was right. Kinky shit going down here.

I read it out.

"Now we know why Griffin wanted to see Pascal," Quinn says.

"Like I give a fuck about Griffin," I say, walking up to Pascal. I hand her back her phone, and then duck down in front of her. The girl winces but doesn't back away. She instantly goes up in my estimation. Although I also want to scream at her for not coming to me sooner, but the logical part of my brain kicks in. She didn't know how to get in touch with me. She only had Lily, and Lily was gone.

"Where did Lily say she thought they had Rebecca?"

Pascal gnaws her lip. "White Jade Casino."

"Motherfucker," Lorcan scowls.

Pascal's eyes widen as she takes in Lorcan and his language. "Is that bad?" she asks.

I don't know what to say to the girl, so I just shake my head and straighten up. The girl is fifteen but she acts younger. When I was fifteen, I was selling pharmaceutical drugs to keep myself off the streets. I was never this young. Ever.

Quinn shakes her head at Pascal. "It's not bad. It's good. You did good. Now come on. Let's find you a room and see if any of my pajamas fit you."

"Quinn," I say.

She looks back.

"Make sure there's no tracker on her phone."

She nods and walks out after Pascal.

I wait until they're out of the room to stalk over to my wardrobe to find some appropriate wear for slaughtering every last one of Kato's men.

"What are you doing?" Lorcan asks, watching me strap a nine-inch blade to my thigh.

"I'm going to the fucking casino, what does it look like?" I snap.

"Shouldn't we wait for the trade?" Dino asks.

Oh, the trade. I shake my head. "Could be a trap. We know where she is, and I'm not sitting here while we discuss battle strategies. I'll go alone if I have to." The violence in my blood has reached boiling point. I could bend steel if I wanted, I'm that pissed off.

All this fucking time, Kato was playing us while we were pointing fingers at Griffin.

I'm going to slice the fucker into ribbons.

Both Dino and Lorcan stare at me, frowns marring their faces. "The place is rigged with cameras. You won't be able to walk in and out without hell breaking loose," says Lorcan.

I give them both a dark smile. "Then let it fucking break loose."

TWENTY-FOUR

LORCAN

"JUST GIVE us one night to plan," I say to Viola.

"Fuck off," is her response.

The demonic look on her face tells me she's not listening. She's strapping all kinds of weapons to her body. Knives, long and short. Ones for throwing. There's even a holster of fucking throwing stars. I shake my head when she pulls out the crossbow.

I glance at Dino. "Don't let her leave."

His brow knits in the middle. "And how the fuck do you expect me to do that?"

"Whatever it takes," I say as I stride out the door.

I've seen Viola make rash decisions. I've seen her react with violence. But I've never seen her be a slave to her emotions. She's pissed, but also hurting. The pain in the depths of her eyes is clouding her judgment. I need to stop her.

Fucking hell.

Dante needs to stop her.

She only seems to listen to that dickhead lately.

I find him in the gym running hard. The sweat is pouring off him. The bastard is ripped. No wonder Viola has wet fucking dreams for this guy. He's a goddamn machine.

"Rebecca's been found," I say, slightly out of breath. I hate myself for having to lean against the wall, sucking air in like a bloody fish.

"Where?" Dante asks as he stops running, frowning as he takes his earphones out.

"White Jade Casino. Viola's getting ready to raze it to the fucking ground," I say, finally catching my breath.

He nods, casually grabbing his water bottle and towel from a side bench like we're at some kind of holiday resort.

"You need to stop her."

"I don't need to do anything," he says, knocking back a swig of his bottle.

I glare at him. "She's going to get herself killed."

"If you think that, then you don't know *our* girl."

I'm still breathing hard, so I take a few seconds to gather myself. Then I walk right up to him. "I don't get you. You act like you care about her but all you care about is yourself."

He smirks at me, dabbing his face with that fucking towel.

"Dante!" Viola stalks into the gym as he looks up. She's wearing a black, ballerina skirted, cocktail dress with black high heeled boots. She's also carrying a semi-automatic pistol in one hand and a crossbow under the arm of the other. Her ponytail swishes, and flashes of her knives show under her skirt as she walks toward us.

She looks fucking divine.

"Get dressed," she says to him. "You too, if you're coming with us." She looks at me, just as Dino appears and raises his palms up when he sees me. He has on a black suit jacket with the tell-tale sign of a concealed gun under it.

"Don't fucking try and explain it," I say to him. I don't want to know.

Ten minutes later, we're all in Dante's fucking car heading toward a massacre.

"Please tell me there's a plan," I say.

Viola looks over her shoulder. "Find my mother and Lily, kill anyone who tries to stop us."

Dante sighs. "What she means is you both stay in the car. Keep your phones on. Be ready to drive as soon as we tell you to."

"Like fuck am I staying in the car," I say to him.

"Fine. We just need one of you to drive" He looks at Dino in the rearview mirror. "You stay in the car."

Dino scowls but nods.

"It makes sense. He's the best fucking driver we've got," says Viola, like we're discussing a fucking rally drive or some shit.

By some miracle we make it to the casino without getting pulled over by the police for speeding. Dino takes the wheel and pulls the car away from the entrance where valet parking is, and into the pick-up and drop off area. Then all three of us walk toward the casino.

Viola, thank fuck, has put the crossbow inside a violin case that she found in the music block.

"We're the entertainment for the night," she says flirtatiously to the doorman holding the violin case with her good hand. The dress is a plunge neck, so her tits are almost out for all the world to see. It works in her favor and the doorman allows us in without question. As soon as we're inside, she makes a beeline for the bar.

Dante stops me from following her. "Play the tables. Look like you're drunk. We need you to be our eyes and ears on the floor. No surprises. Anyone comes in that door you don't like the look of, you know what to do."

Clenching my jaw, I nod. Act drunk. I can do that. The rest of it? Fucking psycho talk.

I grab a passing drink off a waiter's tray as soon as Dante stalks off in the direction Viola went. The urge to follow her into the lion's den is fucking overwhelming. Why am I even listening to Psycho Charlie anyway? Because he's a fucking hired gun and does this for a living. I've killed before, but under duress. Not on a whim because I don't like the look of someone.

This is fucking crazy.

I need to trust that he can keep her safe.

After the longest ten minutes of my life, where every person walking through that goddamn door is someone I might have to take out, my phone vibrates.

I walk off to the side to answer it.

"We've got her. Viola's taken the rear exit and will meet you out front," says Dante.

I pocket my phone, down my drink, and walk out the front doors of the casino.

There's no sign of the Mustang until I hear it roar around the corner like a souped-up street racer. That's Dino behind the wheel alright. He jerks to a stop right in front of me.

"Where are they?" I say, after getting in.

"Who the fuck knows, I went around the back but I didn't see them."

I scrub a hand over my face as we drive past the front entrance and several men storm out of the casino. They run down the steps, opening fire right at the Mustang.

"She's not here. Try around the back again" I say. "So fucking glad this isn't my McLaren," I mutter as bullets hit the car and Dino takes a hairpin corner, screeching into an exit only back route.

Viola, with an older lady who must be Rebecca, bursts around the side of the back entrance just as we career into the delivery drop off area and slam on the brakes.

"Where the fuck were you?" Viola hisses as she helps Rebecca climb in the back seat and then runs around to the other side.

"Where's Dante?"

Viola shakes her head. "He's not coming."

"What the fuck? Why?" Dino exclaims just as another fucking bullet explodes the rear window, covering everyone in glass.

"Just go!" Viola orders.

"Is he dead?" Dino can't help but ask.

I shoot him a look but Viola isn't upset by his question.

"No. He's fine. He's holding them off for us. We need to go now," Viola snaps. Thank fuck after that, Dino doesn't wait. He accelerates and the car screams like a banshee out of the casino parking lot.

Dino drives like hell is chasing him, and after a few miles I have to tell him to chill the fuck out or we'll get pulled over by the police. I didn't notice before, but I see it now. Viola is covered in blood. The last thing we need are the cops questioning us.

Viola is staring straight ahead, looking white as a sheet, while Rebecca holds her hand in a death like grip. Rebecca hasn't said a word the entire time. Apart from her hair which is darker, Rebecca looks like Viola. She has the same eyes.

"Is your mum okay?" I say to Viola after we've slowed down and we're sure no one is following us.

"She's fine. This is how she is. Sometimes she doesn't talk," Viola says, jaw clenched as she holds her mother's hand.

"Where's Lily?" Dino asks, glancing up at the rearview mirror.

It only dawns on me then that Lily is fucking missing.

Viola shakes her head. "She wasn't there. Dante went to look for her, so we got separated. He's going to join us later."

I nod, choosing to keep my concerns to myself. Dante can take care of himself. Of that I've no fucking doubt.

When we get back to the school, Quinn looks after Rebecca just like she did with Pascal. Quinn is a goddamn saint. I've no idea why she's putting up with us all and sticking around, but I'm grateful. She reminds me of Saskia in a way. Fuck, I need to call my sister. I haven't spoken to her in weeks.

I take myself off outside to one of the quads and dial her number.

"You've got to be kidding me. It's 2 a.m. in the morning, Lor. Who died? Because that's got to be the reason you're interrupting my beauty sleep," Saskia growls down the phone.

I chuckle. "Goddamn. It's so nice to hear your voice."

"So, no one died?"

"Dante, maybe," I say in a lowered tone.

"Good fucking riddance. I hate that man. He tried to kill me once, remember?"

"How could I forget," I say darkly. But I did forget. It's all just fucked up. That's the reality of it. When Viola was out of my life, I knew what I was doing, and what I was aiming for. And now she's back in it, I'm in a fucking hurricane being dragged in a thousand different directions. And the eye of the storm, namely Viola, keeps on pulling me back to the middle of it all.

"Poetic, brother. Is that your wedding speech?"

I snort. I must have said that out loud. *Fuck me I'm tired.*

"We should meet up soon."

"Only if you bring Viola. My girl time has been severely lacking since you left me in this hell hole of a school to go off and single-handedly run Joseph's empire."

I say goodnight and hang up, and then walk back into the dorms. Being back here has some dark memories attached. I'll be glad when that psycho converts this place into an apartment complex. This dump needs a facelift, and a new soul for that matter. Before Viola got here it was fucking pitch black.

I'm about to take my usual spot on the sofa when the door to Viola's room opens. "In here," she says, jerking her head to indicate I come inside her room.

I give her a look to make sure. She's washed the blood from her face and she's wearing some of Quinn's pajamas. A set with cats on the front and words that say, 'Cats Sleep Anywhere…Like Me'. It's too fucking cute.

With a sigh I follow her into her room. I'm not so surprised to see Dino already in the bed. Viola crawls into the middle of it, beside Dino, leaving a space to the right. I take that as my cue to join them, undressing as I walk toward the side that's empty. I drop a kiss on her shoulder as I ease myself in behind her. She's got her ass sticking out of the bedsheets and her face on Dino's chest. She sighs as I slip a hand up her pajama top and squeeze her breast, just like I always used to.

Immediately, I'm hard.

"I'm not in the mood to fuck," she mumbles.

I kiss the back of her neck. "I know, sweetheart," I say.

But after a minute, she pushes back against me, rubbing herself all over my cock.

"I thought you said you weren't in the mood?" I say in a low voice.

She sighs. "I wasn't but now I want you both."

"I think Dino is asleep," I say, softly.

"We could wake him?" she says, sounding out of it herself.

"No, don't," I whisper. "Don't make a sound. I want you to myself." I slip my hand down the front of her pajama pants to the sweet spot between her legs. She's soaking wet. She moans lightly as I kiss the back of her neck and move my mouth to her earlobe. There's a delicious noise she makes when I plunge my fingers into her tight pussy and fuck her with them until she's trembling.

"Lor, fuck me. I need you to make me come hard."

"Oh, I'll make you come hard, but you'd better not make a sound," I say to her.

I draw her face to me, stealing her breath away with a kiss. Her eyes flash with heat in the low light, but all she does is bite my tongue and moan louder. When I stick a finger in her mouth to shush her, she bites that too.

She told me not to treat her like she was dead. This is what I've been wanting to do to her since I saw her at the casino. Viola is mine. She always has been.

Ours.

Even Dante said it. How I ended up sharing her with him I'll never fucking know. But all that matters is that she's here with me now.

Where she belongs.

I never should have let her go.

Keeping my hand over her mouth to keep her quiet, I drag her pajama bottoms down. I grip my cock and line it up between her ass cheeks. Her wet heat, the way she squirms in my arms…*Fuck.* It just entices me even more. I tease her entrance first, making her gasp beneath my fingers. Then I ease my cock inside her. She clenches around me as I start to move my hips ever so fucking slowly. And once I'm buried deep in her pussy, she starts to moan again.

"Shut the fuck up," I berate her in a hushed voice.

I've no longer got a hand over her mouth. Instead, I've tangled it in the thick of her hair, yanking it. She arches her back, sucking me down deeper, making me wish Sinner wasn't in the fucking bed with us and I could take her as hard and as fast as I please.

I'm caught up in the feel of her moving, tight around my dick, when Dino fucking wakes up.

"You pair of fucking assholes," he grumbles.

Fucking finally. The restraint was driving me nuts.

"You were asleep," I say.

Viola laughs lightly. "Just shut the hell up and kiss me, Sinner." Reluctantly, I pull out as she climbs on top of him. I move behind her and lift her pajama top off, dropping kisses onto the dip of her neck, massaging my hands over her breasts.

Dino stops grumbling as she bends away from me and down to kiss him. Then she adjusts lower to take him in her mouth. He closes his eyes, resting his head back onto the pillow.

The sight of her sucking his cock pushes me over the fucking edge. I grab her hips, rubbing my cock at her dripping entrance. She pushes back against me, telling me what she wants. I don't hesitate. I slam into her like I've been needing to this entire time and then fuck her relentlessly. She gives off a muffled yelp but doesn't stop grinding and fucking Dino's cock with her mouth.

This is where our angel belongs.

In our hearts, and in our fucking bed.

TWENTY-FIVE

VIOLA

I'M NOT good with kids or catatonic mothers. I shamelessly leave Quinn to deal with both Pascal and Rebecca the next day. Lorcan and Dino seem to have slipped back into how things used to be in the frat house. At least that's how it feels. Lorcan cooks me breakfast, Dino brings me coffee.

It's nice.

But Lily is still missing, Dante hasn't come home, and Jude is still in Juvie.

And Adrien and Kristian are also still very much alive.

"I checked with Quinn. There's no sign of him," says Dino, taking a seat next to me in the cafeteria of the school. "Here," he says, sliding a latte over to me. There's a kitchenette in the boarding house, but the main cafeteria has a proper coffee machine. It also has one wall of sliding glass doors that open onto a view of the lake. It's a good place to drink coffee and decide who to kill next.

Dino is looking at me, waiting for me to respond.

"Dante said he'd come back," I say. "So he will." I don't know why I feel the need to explain Dante's actions or defend him, but I do.

Dino nods. "I believe you."

I look at him blankly. "So, are you and Lor staying?" I guessed as much after last night. Things have become messy again between us. And while I adore messy, I don't like complicated.

"I said I'd never leave you," Dino says, resting a hand on my knee. I don't flinch, or feel the urge to slice his dick off, so that's progress. "About last night…"

"I'm not going to break, I told you that."

"I just want to make sure that you're fine. Because if you're not ready—"

"If you don't stop talking, I'll cut your tongue out," I say in a mild tone. I appreciate the boys being cautious, I do. They're allowed to be. I just want them to stop fussing and help me kill the people who deserve to die.

Dino puts his cup down, takes my coffee out of my hands, and then takes my hands in his.

"I told you before, I'm not leaving you. Ever," he says, his baby blue eyes looking deep into mine.

"I treat you like shit," I say to him.

He smirks. "Sometimes. And other times you blow my mind."

"That blowjob was a one time deal," I say. "I felt sorry for you."

He chuckles. "You can feel sorry for me whenever you like."

There's a noise at the far side of the room where the entrance is. I glance up to see Pascal standing at the doors. She's still shit scared of me.

Dino straightens and waves her in. "Pascal, are you okay? Did you want something?"

"Quinn sent me to get her a coffee," she says.

Dino nods and gets to his feet. "Come on, let me show you how to make a blinding cup of coffee."

I take the opportunity to leave the cafeteria. It's getting too crowded, and I need some air.

I slaughtered a handful of Kato's men last night before he escaped, but the itching under my skin hasn't gone away. They were quick deaths that I had little or no control over. Kills like that have never quenched my 'thirst'. The release I desire is harder to satisfy. It's becoming more and more elusive. I'm the monster my father always wanted me to be.

Cold.

Dark.

And alone.

As much as Dino says he will never leave me, he will. Dante has, so why not the others? And they did before. I pushed them away and they left. How much longer can I keep up this pretense that I'm fine?

Quinn is working at her computer when I walk into her office and take a seat on one of the chintzy sofas. "Where's Rebecca?"

"I left her in the upstairs lounge watching daytime TV. I had some work to do."

"I don't expect you to babysit, you know," I say.

Quinn nods. "I know, but the last thing you need right now is to worry about your mother. I've got her. That's why I'm here. You just focus on what you need to do next."

So many people around me give up their lives for me. I never asked for it.

Dante was right.

Charisma makes others drawn to me whether I like it or not. He said that when he was trying to make me read another one of his damn books. What I wouldn't give to have him here, lecturing me on reading more.

"Dante hasn't got in touch, has he?" I ask Quinn.

She shakes her head. "No, his phone is off grid." She frowns when she looks at me. "Are you worried about him?"

"I don't know," I say honestly.

"It's not the first time he's gone missing," she says. Suddenly, she narrows her eyes. "You slept with him, didn't you?"

I don't know what to say to that, so I say nothing.

"Jesus, Viola, is no one off limits to you?" she says, brows raised. Then she sighs. "I guess it's been on the cards for a while. Just be careful. As I said before, he's no good for you."

I open my mouth to respond but then Pascal walks in with a black coffee for Quinn.

Irritation suddenly spikes in my veins. No one is moving fast enough today. It's infuriating. And I can't wait for Dante any longer.

If he's even coming back.

"Pascal," I say. "Can I borrow you for a minute?"

Quinn frowns at me but I don't give her a chance to get involved. As soon as Pascal follows me outside, I take her on a walk with me around the perimeter to check for security breaches. It needs to be done. Dante has been doing it since we got here. I could ask one of the boys, but I feel like doing it myself.

Pascal is pretty quiet so that suits me fine as I check the windows and the exits. No one knows we are here, but break-ins happen all the time. It wouldn't do to be caught off guard either, if any of my father's men turn up.

"I need to borrow your phone," I say to her.

She hesitates but then takes her phone out and hands it to me.

I immediately call Griffin.

"Pascal, where are you?" It's a woman's voice. A harsh one. Not Griffin

"It's Viola, not Pascal. Is Griffin there?"

There's muffled arguing and then Griffin comes on the phone. "You caused quite the upset last night. All I keep hearing about is the carnage you and your blue-eyed demon did at White Jade."

Blue-eyed demon. It's Kato's name for Dante.

"Do you have Lily?"

"Kristian has her."

"And Dante?"

There's silence at the other end of the line. "Have you lost your demon already? Maybe your father's made him a deal he can't refuse this time, now that Rebecca is safe?"

Doing everything I can not to grind my teeth down the phone, I chew the inside of my lip instead. "Just meet me in the old derelict church in Whitechapel at 8 p.m. I want Lily back and Jude protected. In exchange you get your niece back safe and sound."

"That's two for one. That won't fly with Kristian. He doesn't care about my niece."

"But you care about her? Make it worth his while."

"But Kristian—"

"Kristian can go fuck himself," I snap. Dante's words echo in my mind. *Make him useful.* I suck in a breath and offer Griffin a deal in exchange for putting his lot in with me. He wants Kato's gun business. I can give him that once I've gotten rid of Adrien and Kristian. Dante is always telling me I need allies.

"Fine," he says gruffly. "I can get you Lily in exchange for my niece. I'll tell Kristian we're making a trade with Kato. He'll buy that."

"And Jude?"

"I'll speak to my boys."

After I hang up, Pascal looks at me, her eyes brimming with what look like tears.

"You'll be going home soon," I say.

"That's just it. I'd rather die than go back to my uncle," she says dramatically, and then runs off into the middle of the sports pitch. She's fucking fast too for a fifteen-year-old.

For fuck's sake. Why can't I catch a break?

TWENTY-SIX

VIOLA

SHOULD I run after her or send one of the boys? I stare at her retreating form until she stops dead in the middle of the field and sits down, butt on the long grass, head between her knees. If she's crying again...

I drag in a breath and make the long walk toward the center of the pitch. By the time I get there, I'm cursing her under my breath. The field is wet and muddy and it's starting to fucking rain again.

Her shoulders are shaking, but she's not making any noise. Is she crying? I don't know what to do so I tentatively stand next to her and put a hand on her shoulder.

"Please don't make me go back there." After a few seconds she adds. "He comes into my room at night."

Fucking bastard.

"If you don't want to go back, you can stay here," I say, instantly regretting the words that are coming out of my mouth. I can't even look after myself, never mind a teenage girl. "Although Quinn will have to look after us both because I suck at it," I say.

After a few seconds, Pascal looks up at me. "You promise?"

I hate making promises I can't keep.

But I need her to stop crying and come in from the rain.

"I promise," I say. "But let's keep this between us for now."

After Lorcan cooks everyone dinner in the canteen kitchen, I make my way to my room to get dressed for the trade. Pascal has agreed to come with me as long as I don't leave her behind once we've got Lily. Maybe I should feel guilty for using her as bait, but what else can I do? I can't leave Lily in Kristian's hands. And I can't just sit and do nothing. I'm used to taking control. I need to do something to keep my darkness sated because if I don't, I might just go a little stir crazy.

Dante. Where the fuck are you?

And why the hell does Lily keep getting herself kidnapped? Once she gets here, we're going to have words. Maybe Dante can train her a little to make sure she's not unnecessarily putting herself at risk.

If Dante comes back.

I don't even know if he's alive. But if he was dead, Griffin would have rubbed it in my face. Maybe I shouldn't have told him about his parents. He was so dismissive about the information I gave him. Was he never fucking curious? Adrien killed his mother and his father, and then turned him into a monster just like me.

Adrien did this to him. To me. To us.

I wouldn't be like this if Adrien hadn't molded me. My whole life has been test after fucking test. He pushed me so far to see if I would break.

"You can let him fuck you, take your virginity, or you can gut him like a fish," Adrien says. I've just turned fourteen. This isn't the first test, and it won't be the last. But it's the worst one so far.

He places the knife under the pillow next to my head. I can't move my head too much because the drugs have kicked in, but I'm not so far gone that I don't know the choices he's given me.

He's always giving me choices.

And when I choose the right one, I get to live.

After that, Adrien goes. He leaves the light on because he likes to watch through the two-way mirror above my dressing table. I lie on the bed, dipping in and out of consciousness, praying that I can move fast enough to save myself again.

I must have fallen asleep because I wake up to someone breathing heavily over me. It's one of Adrien's friends with peppery hair and dark eyes. He smells of alcohol and cigars. He chuckles as he leans over, his hands sliding up my skirt.

"Such a sweet thing," he says in a gruff voice as he starts pulling down my knickers. My arms feel heavy and my brain too slow to catch up. I try to push him away.

"No, no, no," I say. "Please."

But I'm not strong enough.

"Shush, beautiful, this is going to feel so good," he says, touching my intimate place, making tears leak from my eyes. I try to keep my legs closed but he just pushes them wide.

I move my hand higher under my pillow. The knife is no longer where my father left it. Panic clutches my chest. Where is it? The man fumbles with his trouser zipper and climbs on top, forcing himself between my legs. Gathering what strength I have, I scream and launch myself at him, biting his ear. He roars and smacks me back onto the bed.

There's the sound of metal falling.

The knife!

I turn over and reach for it, but he drags me by my hair, pain erupting at the roots. No, I need to reach it. My fingers graze the edge of the hilt. His hands are on my thighs, crushing them. He flips me over. At the last second, I grab the knife and stick him with the blade again and again and again. Bright red spatters everywhere, until I'm covered in it. Covered in him. He moans, but not with passion.

I'm killing him.

Breathing hard, I give him one final stab as the grief explodes inside my chest. And only then do I stop and cry until I have no more tears left inside me.

I learned later that Adrien sent that man into my room long after the drugs wore off. He said the fear froze me. I couldn't blame nearly being raped on anything but me not reacting fast enough. The next time he sent someone into my room, they got as far as touching me before I knifed them. Until one guy knocked my head against the wall so hard, I almost passed out. After that, I didn't even wait for them to come into my room. I stood behind the door, knife poised.

The only people who could have possibly tried to come into my room without me trying to kill them was the maid and my mother. But Rebecca never left her own room. And the maid was absolutely terrified of me.

Dante, when he returned after college, was the only one who showed me how to channel my anger.

He was tainted by my father just like me, but I sensed he wasn't as broken.

I needed him back then.

Just like I need him now.

The wrench in my chest aches. It's the same one I had when I was locked in that room, waiting for the men to come and hurt me. I don't know how to make it go away without using a knife.

I walk up to the mirror and stare at my reflection until the intensity of staring makes my eyes water. I put everything inside me into those fake tears, trying to cry for once.

But nothing comes out.

Only knives work.

So, I take five of them and strap one to each thigh, and one to each forearm. And then I hide the last one in the small of my back. Then I get dressed in a black t-shirt and a leather skirt, with some black boots, and tie my hair up in a messy bun. *Time to get Lily back and use my knives on anyone who tries to stop me. That's the only thing I'm good for.*

Someone knocks on my door, so I stay very still hoping they'll go away. After a few minutes they do, and I breathe a sigh of relief.

I get my phone out and call the number Griffin gave me when I asked him for it. After a few minutes, Kristian answers.

"Kristian, it's Viola," I say.

"Well, hello, my love, did you miss me?"

"I have a new deal. One that you'll like. But I need to speak to Lily first."

"You don't want much, do you?"

"Lily first," I snap.

"Bossy little bitch," he says. "Tell me about the deal, and then I'll get Lily."

I knew he'd bargain so I go ahead and explain my deal, and after a few seconds he passes the phone to Lily. She's not with Griffin. That's good. As much as Kristian is a sick fuck, he's not into underage girls. That makes him the preferred partner in all of this.

Even if all I want to do is kill him.

"Cousin V!"

"Lily," I say as soon as she comes on the phone. "Can Kristian hear you?"

"Er no," she says. "The bastard is—"

"Don't say anything but yes or no. Do you still have the Liquid E on you?"

"Yes," she says.

"Then do exactly as I tell you."

TWENTY-SEVEN

DINO

I SHOULDN'T BE SMOKING, but fuck it. Life's too short.

I give one last inhale and then stub out my cigarette and toss it into the rose bushes. Ironically, I'm in my old smoking haunt from when we went to school here. Feels fucking weird to be here and not have a teacher come charging around the halls after us. We grew up here, all of us—Lor, Jude, even fucking Finn.

Look at it now.

Rotting away and ready to be knocked down and replaced by some middle class housing community with gates and recycling bins, and management fucking companies.

Just like the first time I saw her, Viola enters the quad.

I smile when I see her. Was it the first time, or was it the second? No matter, she looks absolutely gorgeous as usual. She's staring straight ahead as she walks, not seeing me since I'm hidden from view to the side. I go to call out to her when she stops in the middle and waits. A few seconds later, Pascal joins her wearing her coat and they walk quickly toward the gates of the school where the parking lot is.

As Viola turns down the pathway that leads to the lot, I see her violin case strapped to her shoulder. Except I know that case contains a crossbow.

Fucking hell. What is she up to now?

I have a split second to make a decision. Follow her and keep her out of trouble? Or go back and get Lor.

My curiosity wins and I run after the direction she went. The parking lot is quiet and a little dark when I get there. But then the lights to the Mustang blink on and it reverses toward me. I jump aside and bang on the roof.

The car stops and I stalk up to the driver side and yank open the door. "What the fuck, Viola! Where are you going?"

She glares at me. "Are you following me now?"

"I was smoking in the quad. I saw you leave." I glance across the seat to where Pascal is strapped in. "Please tell me you're going out to get ice cream."

"We're making the trade," says Viola, flicking her eyes heavenward.

"Oh no you're not."

"It's just a fake trade," Pascal tells me with a smile.

"Where?" I ask Viola. As she tells me her plan, I shake my head at her. "This is the worst decision you've ever made. That's not even a plan. It's a stab in the dark."

"Come with, or stay the fuck out of my way," Viola says, also with a smile but not a nice one.

"Ah, for fuck's sake," I say, and open the rear door and get in.

The backseat is icy cold during the drive. Pascal catches me rubbing my hands to keep warm.

"Why is it so cold in here?" she asks.

"Probably because there are no rear or back windows anymore," I say. The rear end is taped up with plastic sheeting. Dante had lots of it in his trunk for reasons I don't care to know about.

Pascal turns a dial on the dash and heat blasts out of the rear facing fans toward me, making it a little less Baltic. "That better?" she asks, turning to look at me.

I give her a nod. "Much better, thank you."

I shoot a look at Viola hoping to fucking God she has a better plan than to just storm the place because if anything happens to this girl, I'll personally hold Viola responsible.

The parking lot next to the church only has a couple of cars in it. Viola passes it by and turns down a darkened lane. She's right to leave the Mustang farther away from the church, but the location she's chosen gives me the creeps.

"No one knows this is here," Viola says when I tell her as much. "And there's a direct route from the church to this road.'

"How did you find this place anyway?" I ask her.

"Jude showed it to me once," she says. She opens the car glove compartment and shoves a gun inside before closing it shut. "Just in case you need an extra one," she says to me.

The plan is for the three of us to enter. Once we have Lily, I'm to get both girls as far away from the church as possible down the route she described.

"I'd prefer for you to leave with the girls," I say to her.

"I'm not leaving here," she says cryptically.

I don't know what she means by that, but I'm loath to ask. No point in arguing with her. I'll just drag her with me when it comes to it. Even if I have to pick her up and carry her out of the fucking church myself.

While we drove here, I sent a discreet message to Lorcan, so the cavalry *is* coming. I just don't know if he'll make it on time.

Viola looks at her watch. "Ready?"

Fuck no, but I let out a breath and get out of the car anyway.

The church is partly boarded-up but most of it is open to the elements. We duck inside and the first thing I notice is the smell of piss mixed with earth and mold. There's a cracked, half standing altar at the end of an aisle of broken benches. Viola walks toward the altar with purpose, leaving Pascal and I to follow her.

When I get halfway down the aisle, Viola ducks down and slides the violin case under one of the pews. Then she gets up off the floor, dusting herself.

"What are you…?"

She shakes her head, finger to her lips, and carries on walking to the end of the aisle. When I reach her, she makes eyes at me and then glances left. I follow her gaze to see a small passageway hidden from the front of the church. That must be the exit around the back of the altar. Viola points and I nod to let her know I understand. I'm just about to ask when my brother is getting here, but I'm saved the trouble.

Kristian and Griffin appear through the broken board, as well as a couple of their men.

"Well, well, well. If it isn't the Brady fucking Bunch." He glances at Griffin. "Kato wants his niece back, really?"

As soon as I hear my fucked-up brother's voice, the urge to smash his mouth in assaults me. I suck in a lungful of air and clench a fist around the handle of the gun Viola gave me. I'm itching to use it.

Viola and Lor were right to have a go at me for not killing Kristian sooner.

I fucked up.

I'm not about to make that same mistake again. I've been throwing my dice every fucking day and every time it lands on double four, it reminds me I need to kill the bastard. Sometimes it doesn't, but I ignore those times.

"Stop right there. Don't come any closer," Viola calls over to the men.

"Where's Lily?" I shout.

"Impatient as ever baby brother." Kris grins and a few seconds later another heavy of Kristian's turns up holding Lily hostage.

I release a breath when I see her. There's a bruise on her face and her lip is busted, but she's alive.

"I'm okay. But this fucker has the worst breath in the wo—" Lily says earning herself the slam of a gun butt to the head. "Oww," she exclaims.

"Shut your mouth, you fucking cunt," the guy snarls, grabbing a handful of her hair and jerking her head back with it.

I start forward, but Viola stops me with her arm in front. There's a dangerous glint in her eyes that only I can see.

"Send her to the middle of the aisle and we'll do the same with Pascal," Viola says, looking back up to where Kristian and Griffin are standing.

Griffin nods at the man holding Lily.

"Viola," says Kristian, in a dangerous voice. "This isn't the trade we discussed."

Griffin frowns and I shoot a look at Viola. "What's he talking about?" I say.

She looks at me with glazed eyes. "I told you, I'm coming back."

I shake my head. "No, no. That's not what you told me in the car."

"I lied to you. This is the only way to save Jude. They won't hurt him if I marry Kristian willingly."

I look between my brother and Viola in disbelief. Kristian is grinning like the cat who got the cream. And Viola is giving me a blank look like she doesn't fucking care. Griffin's frown deepens and he shifts from foot to foot.

"But we're getting Jude out," I say, jaw clenched. There's a heaviness in my throat and nausea in my gut. My aim with the gun wavers. This is all wrong.

"It's too late," she says.

She takes Pascal's hand and together they walk to the middle of the aisle. The man holding Lily lets her go. Lily stumbles forward, throws a middle finger at him, and then carries on toward Viola and Pascal.

They meet in the middle. Viola hugs Lily briefly and then

pushes her away. Pascal wastes no time, darting forward, grabbing Lily's hand and dragging her to the floor.

At the same time, Viola opens fire with the knives strapped to her arms. She kills the man who was holding Lily and one of the other guards instantly, and dives for her crossbow.

I have no idea what's going on, but Pascal and Lily have crawled to the side already and are exposed, so I aim my gun and shoot the third heavy in the shoulder before he can get to them. He's not dead, but Viola nods my way in silent thanks, causing warmth to bloom in my chest.

By the time Pascal and Lily have reached the end of the pew and disappeared out of the church, we're at a stalemate.

Maybe this was Viola's plan all along.

Although Viola has her crossbow now and it's pointed at Griffin, not Kristian. I shift my aim between him, the remaining guard, and my brother. No one moves but…*what the fuck is going on?*

Kristian is laughing, pissing himself actually. "That's the funniest thing I've seen all fucking week." He wipes away an imaginary tear. "My dear, you are delightful. I can't wait until our wedding night."

"She's not marrying you," I say.

"Oh, but she is. She called me and offered herself willingly if I left the girls and her convict boyfriend alone." He gives a shrug. "The keys to the empire in exchange for a show of faith. He reaches into his pocket and pulls out his own gun and shoots Griffin point blank. While Viola shoots the remaining guard in the head with her bow.

"Now your juvie boyfriend is safe, and we're alone," Kristian says, eyes almost black in the low light.

My heart is racing, and my mouth is fucking dry. What just happened?

"Viola? What the fuck is going on?" I ask.

"Griffin was molesting Pascal. That's why he wasn't interested in me sexually. So I struck a deal with Kristian." She tosses her crossbow onto a bench and walks toward my brother who puts an arm around her like he owns her.

"Take the girls back to the car," she says.

I keep my gun trained on Kris. I don't trust him. "I don't understand. Why are you going with him," I say.

"Go, check on the girls," she hisses.

I shake my head. "I'm not leaving you with him."

Viola glares at me and then turns to Kristian and fucking kisses him. It's like I'm in some kind of trance watching her.

My phone starts vibrating in my pocket. I ignore it, dropping the gun to my side while Viola moans into Kristian's mouth. Kristian opens his eyes and smirks as he devours her in return. I can't not look even though the sight of them makes my stomach roil.

Why they fuck is she kissing him?

It's got to be a mistake.

Suddenly he chokes, eyes glazing over as he slumps in her arms.

"I thought the drugs Lily gave him would never fucking kick in," she says, wiping her face with her sleeve, pushing Kristian onto the floor while she steps away from him.

I stare at my brother.

Is he even breathing?

Viola starts to drag my brother down the aisle. She doesn't get very far. She almost stumbles. I don't miss the shaking of her legs as she steadies herself. I'm at her side in seconds. She pushes me away.

She doesn't need me.

"Don't. Just go and check on the girls."

"Why did you kiss him?" *Why the fuck am I asking that now?*

She gives a little laugh. "I had a little opiate mixed in with my lipstick. Sped up his reaction to the date rape drug." She looks at me. "Don't worry, I took Naloxone to counter the effect before-hand. I'm not going to pass out."

Her eyes are bright and her pupils extra-large. Her lips are smeared red from the lipstick she rubbed off. She looks a little fucked despite her precautions.

"Viola…" The rest of the words die in my throat as I see the expression on her face. The snarl on her face is sin itself. I'm reminded of a wounded but also very dangerous tiger I saw in a zoo once. You do not confront a creature like that. Not if you want to keep your fucking arm.

I stand there as she bends down to strip my brother until he's completely naked. Then she takes a roll of tape out of her pocket and starts taping up his arms and legs.

"Viola," I repeat.

"Get the girls and take them home," she says, eyes dark, face void of emotion. The whole time she's just looking at Kristian.

"Why? What are you going to do to him?"

Viola breaks her gaze away from my brother to stare at me, an evil look creeping onto her face. *Beautiful fucking crazy.*

"Anything I want. Now go. I promised Lorcan you wouldn't see this."

TWENTY-EIGHT

VIOLA

DINO IS LOOKING at me like I'm about to bite his head off and eat him for dinner. I might just do that. The darkness inside of me is a fucking storm brewing. If I don't let it out, it'll consume me. But unlike all the times before when the Devil has come knocking, demanding blood—I'm calm.

Dino doesn't leave until I pick up the crossbow and point it at him. Finally, he gets it and leaves down the side pathway. As soon as we're alone, I drop the bow. The floor of the church is filled with debris and dead leaves which rustle as I kneel down. I tilt my head, breathing in deeply and out as I close my eyes.

The whispers inside my head are the loudest they've ever been.

This kill is mine, all mine. I've earned it.

I don't bother trying to move Kristian again. I wanted him at the altar, a fitting end to him, in my mind—it was a wedding he wanted after all. But my wrist is still broken. I just use what I have. He's drugged. He's not going to be able to move. *Shame.* I like my men to be awake when I carve my love into their hearts.

As the trees rustle and the cold of the night draws in, I bend down and get to work with my knife.

Blood, blood, and more blood.

Against the dirty tiled floor of the church, it's pretty.

He wakes up halfway in, screaming as I dig my nails into his flesh. He's begging me to kill him.

"Shhhhhh," I say, pushing a slick, wet, red finger against his lips. He's crying. Crying isn't enough. I shove the blade in deeper, making him scream again instead. The release comes like a tsunami as soon as I see the fear in his eyes.

I haven't killed him…yet.

But I'm close.

He knows it too.

"I'm s…sorry, Viola. I can't let you do this to him," says a choked-up voice behind me. "I can't ignore the dice."

What dice?

I spin around at the sound and see my savior like a white knight I don't fucking need or want. "He's still my brother," he says, eyes gleaming in the moonlight, wet with tears.

I don't understand what he's saying until it's too late. He raises the gun and pulls the trigger, blowing a hole in Kristian's head, killing him outright.

That was *my* kill.

Rage chokes my chest, and a scream erupts from my throat. I launch myself at Dino, slashing and screaming…anything to take the pain away. And he just stands there and doesn't try to stop me, embracing me.

It takes all of them to pull me off him. He's soaked in blood. Eyes closed. And he's not moving.

Dino.

No, no, no…

A strong arm locks around my waist, and a firm hand circles my undamaged wrist preventing me from moving it. Someone hauls me to the other side of the church carcass, squeezing hard so I drop the knife. The sharp tang of blood sticks in my throat as I try to speak. No words come out. None.

My chest is tight, my heart raw. Chlorine and ash, the smell of it, draws sanity back from somewhere lost inside.

"V, you need to come back to me."

It's Dante who has me.

"Dino," I croak, feeling a dam burst in my core and all the pain flood into every part of my body. I'm limp in his arms. *Lost in them.* "Dino?" I ask, desperate, watching Lorcan pump his chest and give him the kiss of life. There's blood on Lorcan's hands and face. There's blood all over Dino.

And me.

There's blood everywhere.

"Let's get you out of here," Dante says.

I don't struggle. I let D lead me outside into the blackness of the night where a car is waiting. I squint at the brightness of the headlights as they flash in my face as I walk numbly to the car. It's Dante's Mustang. For once, I'm glad to see the shitty brown color. It's like a forgotten memory from a long time ago coming back to reassure me. Dante ushers me inside, reaches across to take his keys out the ignition. Then he's gone, leaving me in the dark.

I didn't kill him.

The light didn't leave his eyes.

Blue eyes filled with love as I thrust the blade in, haunt me. I wait in the cab of the car while sirens wail in the distance and think of nothing but his eyes. I look down at my hands. They're bloody, although some of it has dried already and caked under the nails. I feel empty. I glance out of the window at the empty lamp lit streets. Empty. Like me. There's no Devil inside me right now. I don't know where it went but it left a hole in my heart and a gnawing in the pit of my stomach.

I didn't kill him.

Did I?

Fuck. I kick the dash. *Fuck this shit. Fuck this SHIT!* I ram the front of the dash with my foot a few times until the driver side door swings open.

"V! Find your fucking zen and hold onto it, will you?" snaps Dante.

"You find your fucking zen!" I shout at him. "Where were you?!" Where was he when I needed him? He fucking left me.

Look at what I did. This is what I was afraid of.

Dante slams the door in my face, leaving me to dig my nails into the worn leather and squeeze my eyes shut.

Why the fuck did Dino come back? Why was he talking about fucking dice?

After a minute, the driver side door swings open, and Dante gets in the car. He starts it and drives off. I can't help but look out of the window to see…*To see fucking what? Dino's body being carried out of the church? They're going to burn it. Burn the fucking church down to the ground. Leave nothing for them to find.*

Smoke curls into the sky as I knew it would.

"Are they burning the evidence?" I ask my old mentor. My throat feels like I've swallowed a vat of acid. My heart is pounding like I've run a thousand miles.

"He's still alive," Dante says after a few seconds of silence. "But only just. Lorcan and Finn are taking him to St Guys."

They're taking him to the hospital. Dino is alive for now. I breathe out, long and hard, letting all the pain flow with it. But then it rushes back in when I fill my lungs up and squats in my throat. *What the fuck is wrong with me?*

I drop back against the seat, my good hand gripping the leather and my fucked one in my lap. All the anger has gone again, just as quickly as it came.

"You're losing control," Dante says, after a mile or so of tranquility.

I shake my head. "No. I've been feeling more in control these last few weeks. This is just what I am," I snort.

"Are you?" Dante asks. "Or is that the excuse you're telling yourself?"

"Fuck you," I say, staring straight ahead. "Where were you?"

Dante tosses a file onto my lap. It's the file I found in my father's house. "I was busy confirming what you told me. And you know why? Because not every fucking thing revolves around you."

I pick up the file, leaving bloody red handprints all over it. The sight of Dino's blood makes me drop the file on the floor.

"Take me to St Guys," I say.

"You are not going anywhere near that boy until you've cleaned yourself up. Do you want to go to prison?"

I close my eyes. "Maybe I should."

Dante snorts a laugh. "Always about you. You're not even thinking about the rest of us."

"Sounds like we have a lot in common," I say. The adrenaline is leaving my system. I'm exhausted.

I'm also dead fucking cold inside.

Just like what you did to Dino?

TWENTY-NINE

VIOLA

DANTE DRIVES us to Sacred Heart. He leaves me to clean up, but I don't. I just stand there and stare at my face in the bathroom mirror. My face is streaked in blood. My hair is pink, stained with it. I must have touched my hair at some point.

I zone in and out until I'm aware of voices downstairs—Lorcan's and Dante's. The walls are so thin here, I can hear them perfectly. Even better if I crack open the door.

"—not communicating with his lawyer anymore."

"So what are you going to tell her?"

"I'm not telling her shit until we fucking know what's going on."

"Killing Griffin was a mistake."

"You don't think I know that. They have him, I'm sure of it."

I've heard enough.

"Who has who?" I ask, walking out of the bedroom to peer over the banister.

Lorcan's eyes blaze when he looks up and sees me, and then he jerks his gaze away. He shakes his head in that nonchalant way of his.

"I can't look at you right now, Viola," he says.

I shoot a look at Dante who casually raises a brow. "I told you to get cleaned up."

"I want to go to St Guys," I stress at him.

"So you said, get cleaned up first."

I regard him coolly for a few moments then turn back to my room, leaving the door open so I can still eavesdrop.

"She's not going anywhere near that hospital," Lorcan says.

"Oh, I know."

Someone sighs. Lorcan possibly. "The lawyers are doing what they can but until we get an update from the warden, it's likely his family has had him ghosted or moved to a more solitary unit."

"She'll find out."

"I'll tell her after Dino is back on his feet. Jude going silent is the last thing she needs. Right, I need to go to the hospital. I left Finn to guard the door while I brought the girls back."

"I'll make sure she stays here."

I move away from the door as Lorcan departs and Dante goes into Quinn's office. I make a snap decision to grab my coat and quietly leave after Lorcan out the front entrance.

I'm about to chase after him when I feel the presence of someone. On the veranda is Rebecca in a chair with a blanket around her. I walk up to my mother and drop a kiss on her frail body, breathing in her scent. I feel absolutely nothing when I do, but it feels right to do it.

Lorcan's car is gone by the time I get to the parking lot. I'm fine with that. I wasn't looking forward to convincing him to take me with him anyway. The Mustang is parked where it always is. I break in easily and hot wire it. Then I drive as fast as the speed limit will let me, all the way to St Guys.

I don't know what I'm hoping for when I get there.

To see Dino? To talk to him. To tell him I'm fucking sorry.

Because I am.

This is all my fault.

I park up in a visitor bay and enter the hospital through one of the underground entrances. There's a few for the emergency crew and they're less likely to stop me and ask why I'm covered in blood.

After wandering aimlessly for a while, I eventually walk up to a reception desk and ask them where I can find Kardinal Vice.

"Second floor, wing 3b. But he's in a private room," says one of the nurses, frowning at me. "I'm sorry, who are you?"

"I'm his fiancée," I say. "I was the one that found him. Excuse me, I need to go and see him now."

"Oh, my gosh, yes of course."

No one stops me going up to the second floor. But the wing has police officers outside of it. I grab a bunch of flowers from an empty room and put my head down as I walk past them. It's only when I get to the area outside the private room, that I see men outside of it I recognize.

My father's men.

And my father with his arm around some woman with bright red hair.

I stall, unable to take a step closer.

The woman with the red hair bursts into tears as the doctor speaks to her. Her face crumples. She half collapses to the floor. "No, no, no. My baby. He's gone. My baby!" she wails. My father picks her up and she buries her head on his shoulder.

Dark dread squeezes my insides until I can't breathe.

Dino can't be dead.

Suddenly, my father looks up. Our eyes connect through the glass of the door. And then my heart literally jumps out of my chest as the phone in my pocket rings. I grab my phone and put it to my ear.

"Why the fuck is Dante telling me you stole his Mustang. Where are you?" It's Lorcan.

"I'm at the hospital," I choke out. The corridor is spinning.

"You're what?! Where?"

"Outside his…his room," I say, blinking rapidly as I look up.

"Viola…" Lorcan says. But I'm not listening.

My father is walking toward the doors.

Turnaround now. You need to leave. He's dead. You can't do anything now.

I turn and walk back the way I came. I don't bother to hold the flowers up. I just keep walking.

"Viola, don't you dare walk away from me," my father calls.

"Viola," Lorcan says again, more gently this time. "Your father has the whole place locked down. You need to leave."

"What do you think I'm doing?" I say. I hang up and keep walking down the white corridors. I've no idea where I'm going. They all look the fucking same.

I just wanted to see him.

Just once.

To say I'm sorry.

Now…It's too late.

Pain. Real pain erodes what's left of me. I keep walking, clawing back the pain until it sticks in my chest and won't leave. I push it down, all the way, making a tight ball of ugliness where no one can find it. It's where I've been shoving it for the last fifteen years, only letting it out when needs must.

Because I'm a fucking monster, just like my father wanted.

When I get outside, the cold air hits me like a slap in the face. Lorcan is striding toward me, concern etched on his features. His eyes are red. He's been crying.

Because Dino is dead.

I killed him.

Internal pain twists and torments my body, making it hard to breathe. Behind me, I hear my father shouting my name, calling me back to him where all is forgiven.

Two paths.

One, a way out. The other, a way in.

But a third opens up as blue and red lights flash and a siren whoops, demanding my attention. Lorcan hesitates, seeing the line of police closing in, his brow is furrowed with fear, grief, and confusion.

Funny how I can read him so clearly now.

I press send on my message to him, which explains every-thing, and then drop Pascal's phone into a potted plant and raise my hands, putting them behind my head.

"Viola Hawkes, you are under arrest on suspicion of manslaughter. You do not have to say anything, but it may harm your defense if you do not mention when questioned something which you later rely on in court…"

Blah, blah, blah.

I close my eyes while they place me in handcuffs. Smiling as the drugs finally kick in to ease the torture, and that my father can't do a fucking thing to get at me now, especially with Griffin dead.

Jude. I'm coming to find you.

———

ALSO BY MALLORY FOX

ABOUT THE AUTHOR

Mallory Fox is addicted to tatted up bad boys, chocolate covered pretzels, and looking deep into heart-melting, big brown eyes... the canine kind.

She loves to write deliciously dark romance with wicked, twisty plots about tainted-love, sweet revenge, and all kinds of emotional-rollercoaster redemption.

Mallory currently lives in London with her bean-shaped dog and the rest of her non-furry family.

Find more Mallory at facebook or sign away your soul at malloryfoxauthor.com/newsletter.

#wickedwordswithheart

Printed in Great Britain
by Amazon